A KILLER
BED & BREAKFAST

Also by Alice Zogg

Stand-Alone Mysteries
A Doomed Reunion
A Lethal Joke
A Dark Book Club
A Bad Apple
Exposing the Past
No Curtain Call
The Ill-Fated Scientist
Accidental Eyewitness
A Bet Turned Deadly

R. A. Huber Mysteries
Evil at Shore Haven
Guilty or Not
Murder at the Cubbyhole
Revamp Camp
Final Stop Albuquerque
The Fall of Optimum House
The Lonesome Autocrat
Tracking Backward
Turn the Joker Around
Reaching Checkmate

A KILLER
BED & BREAKFAST

Alice Zogg

aventine press

This book is a work of fiction.

Published by Aventine Press
1745 La Maderia Dr. SW
Palm Bay, FL 32908
www.aventinepress.com

ISBN: 978-1-955162-38-8
Library of Congress Control Number: 2025912246
Library of Congress Cataloging-in-Publication Data
A Killer Bed & Breakfast/Alice Zogg
Printed in the United States of America

In memory of Casey, a dear fan

CREDITS

Carolyn Weir gave me a glimpse into the many different jobs of a social worker. Her information not only helped with the research of this book, but I learned something along the way. Thank you, Carolyn. I cannot imagine authoring a story without the knowledge that daughter Franziska will proofread my work. Thanks for taking time out from your busy life to do this for me, book after book. Gayle Bartos-Pool is another loyal soul who did not shy away from an editing job. I appreciate your dedication, Gayle. As to the setting of this tale, Castaic Lake had been one of my husband's and my favorite hangouts for many decades, so it was easy to bring the place into my mind's eye. I took the liberty to tweak the State Park a bit, making it fit into my story, but the essence of it is true to date. However, *The Vista* is entirely a product of my imagination.

CAST OF CHARACTERS

Ralph Rhymes Owner of *The Vista*; lacks enthusiasm for the new venture

Kate Rhymes Ralph's spouse and business partner; is excited about their new life

Tim Weinbau A recent graduate of UCLA; rides his bicycle everywhere

Marvel Maxwell A chiropractor; has a sense of humor

Asher Jenkins A young man fresh out of dental school; is on his honeymoon

Norice Jenkins Asher's spouse, a court reporter; is near job burnout

Vigo Castelli A high school teacher; wants to spend time with his brother

Enzo Castelli A sales representative; is about to move out of California

Hien Bong An IT specialist; needs relaxation

Mai Bong Hien's spouse, a home maker; worries about Hien's mental health

Jaqueline Blanchet A social worker; is going through a messy divorce

Clarissa Clever A therapist and Jaqueline's friend; a savvy woman

Martina Padilla Housekeeper at *The Vista*; can learn a lot from a guest room

Amanda Redding Tim Weinbau's girlfriend; is determined to learn the truth

Sheriff Simon Shaft Takes charge; is known for his unorthodox approach to cases

CHAPTER 1

On Sunday night, July 13, all was quiet at *The Vista*, a bed and breakfast near the State Park of Castaic Lake, California. The owners of the idyllic place, Ralph and Kate Rhymes, lay satisfied after lovemaking.

Kate asked, "Are you happy?"

"Sure, it was great," her spouse replied.

"I meant with us living here and running The Vista."

"Oh, that. I guess I'm getting used to it."

He was already half asleep when she mentioned, "We sure had a bunch of nice people here last week. Marvel is staying on for a few more days but everyone else left this evening. A slew of new folks are booked starting tomorrow."

"Uh …yeah…."

Ralph was no longer awake as she rattled on, "Should be interesting. We'll have a young couple on their honeymoon, a middle-aged Vietnamese husband and wife, two brothers, a recent graduate student, and two women friends. Except for the graduate, they've all reserved for the entire week. It's a good thing that we have two rooms available with a couple of twin beds each as both parties, the brothers and the women, requested separate beds."

Realizing that she no longer had an audience, she tried to settle down too, but sleep would not come. Worrying about Ralph kept her mind engaged. She wished that he could become as excited about their venture as she was. They'd opened their doors at the beginning of May, and so far, they'd had full occupancy ever since, with people booked for most of the summer. This came as no surprise since their location was only 40 miles from downtown Los Angeles and accessed via Interstate 5. Their bed and breakfast was just a two-minute walk to Upper Lake Castaic and a seven-mile drive from Magic Mountain.

She had always wanted to run a place like The Vista and was sure that it would become a success story, but Ralph had a tough time adjusting. The reason for their current enterprise was the *faux pas* he'd made in their former lives. For him, their new undertaking was punishment, whereas for her it became a dream come true. She felt certain that The Vista was a gem among bed and breakfast places. She hoped that with time he would also share her enthusiasm.

She sighed and eventually drifted off to sleep.

CHAPTER 2

As each set of guests arrived on Monday, Ralph and Kate welcomed them. Then Kate showed them to their respective rooms and, while doing so, never grew tired of showering the newcomers with information about all the activities available at Lake Castaic.

She addressed each new party with, "There is a swimming beach at the lower lake lagoon, and RV or tent camping is available on the east side of the lagoon with a 24-hour fishing pier nearby. The lower lake is kept to non-power boating, canoeing, kayaking, and of course swimming, whereas at the upper lake you may do power boating, sailing, water-and-jet skiing.

"Bass fishing is year-round in the upper and lower lake, and float-tube fishing in the lower lake. I'm not an angler expert but understand that you can catch striped bass, bullhead, and rainbow trout. Castaic Lake is home to wildlife and countless species of birds with designated trails for bird watching. Enjoy seven miles of trails with spectacular views of Upper Castaic Lake, perfect for mountain biking, backpacking, and horseback riding."

She continued, "I'm sure you noticed the little shed next to our house when you came in. It houses fishing equipment, like casting rods, tackle, bait, and the like. You'll also find trekking poles as well as backpacks there. All of it is at your disposal; just make sure you return the items back where you found them, in clean condition, at the end of the day.

"You saw the dining room as we walked by. Adjacent to it is the recreation room, equipped with a large-screen TV, playing cards, board games, and a small shelf with novels and a few non-fiction books. Guests like to relax there in the evenings.

"We have attached a large map of the lake with its locations of activities to the wall in our main hallway. You can't miss it. Also, if you don't want to walk or drive your car to get around, my husband is available to take you in his golf cart. For a small extra fee, we offer a picnic lunch, but you'll have to let us know by the evening before."

Done with her spiel, Kate left her guests to settle in, reminding them that breakfast was at eight o'clock in the morning but that they could eat earlier if they informed her ahead of time.

Lodgers had arrived at The Vista all day to check in, with Tim Weinbau bringing up the rear in the late afternoon.

He listened to her introduction and then said, "It's all clear to me. Thanks for your hospitality. I'm looking forward to exploring both the upper and lower lake and familiarizing myself with the entire region. I'll take you up on the picnic lunch for tomorrow, but I won't need any transportation as I'll be riding my bike everywhere."

CHAPTER 3

As guests flocked to the dining room on Tuesday morning, the large rectangular table was set for ten people. Norice, the new bride, was surprised when she realized that all would be seated together.

She whispered to Asher, "I had no idea that we are supposed to be one big family."

He muttered, "This is not a hotel restaurant. Did you expect a table for two?"

She giggled and they took their places next to Vigo and Enzo Castelli.

When all guests were seated, their host showed up, offering them coffee, tea, and orange juice. He said, "I'm Ralph Rhymes. We are a small outfit at The Vista. My wife and I own the place and we only have one employee, our housekeeper, Martina Padilla. Currently, the two ladies are cooking breakfast, and while you are waiting to be served, please introduce yourselves to one another, telling a little about who you are and what you expect from your stay here at Castaic Lake."

While listening to him, Clarissa Clever thought, I know this man, but I can't place him for the moment. It will come to me, I'm sure.

Ralph continued, "As to table conversations, anything goes, except what the sign says," and he pointed to a large plaque on the wall portraying people with their raised glasses and the following inscription:

Here's to good conversations galore, but leave politics and religion outside this door.

As Ralph made his exit, the African American man in his 30's seated at the head of the table said, "I might as well start the introductions. I'm Marvel Maxwell, a chiropractor. I was attending a chiropractor and acupuncture convention in Saugus last weekend and couldn't find a room in a nearby hotel. This place here suits me fine, so I'm staying on for a while longer. I'm planning to do lots of fishing here."

Asher spoke for both when he mentioned, "I'm Asher Jenkins and this is my wife Norice. I just graduated from dental school and am excited to join a senior dentist in his practice. Norice is a court reporter. She helped support me through my schooling, I might add. We just got married but didn't want to spend lots of money as we're saving up for a house. So this is our honeymoon. We're planning to go to Magic Mountain one day and hang out at the lake the rest of the week."

The two men seated to their right introduced themselves as Vigo and Enzo Castelli. Vigo was a high school teacher. He wanted to spend some time with his baby brother, Enzo, a sales representative, who planned to move out of California the following week. Tim Weinbau, seated at the foot of the table, simply said that he had just graduated from UCLA last month, that he'd ridden his bike from Sherman Oaks and was looking for some leisure time before starting his job as an electronics technician.

The first-generation Vietnamese couple, Hien and Mai Bong, were next. Hien said, "I'm an IT specialist and my wife is a homemaker. She tells me I'm in need of relaxation."

The woman seated to his left introduced herself, "I'm Jaqueline Blanchet, a social worker. I needed to get away and I'm planning to swim but mostly lay out and relax."

"And I'm Clarissa Clever, a therapist. I came in support of Jaqueline, not in my professional role, but solely as her friend, since she's going through a divorce."

Enzo glanced at Jaqueline and remarked, "I've been there and sympathize. It's not the end of the world, though."

At that point, the Rhimes and their housekeeper carried in an interesting dish of ham, eggs, and cheese scrambled up together; hash brown potatoes; and pancakes topped with fresh strawberries. Everyone helped themselves, then dug in with gusto.

CHAPTER 4

The guests savored their hardy breakfast in silence for a few moments when Vigo, just to make conversation, turned to the UCLA graduate, asking, "So you rode your bicycle all the way from Sherman Oaks? Is that where you live?"

"Yes, on both accounts," replied Tim. "I don't own a car and enjoy riding my bike all over Southern California."

The shy Mai forced herself to ask, "Oh, were you affected by the recent Sherman Oaks brush fire?"

"No. It broke out at the other end of town from where I live."

Asher commented, "These latest fires all over the Southland are not wildfires or forest fires ignited by sparks from electrical wires downed by the Santa Ana winds. They're not acts of God. They were set on purpose."

Clarissa chimed in, "They're under investigation and are most likely the work of the same arsonist, tagged by social media as the Southland Torcher. As far as what is known, the person left no trace behind to date."

Norice, the court reporter, stated, "When they finally catch the perpetrator, he or she will face a murder charge on top of arson, since a firefighter perished in the Malibu blaze."

Marvel spoke up in his deep baritone voice, "I'm glad you said 'he or she.' We think of arsonists as male but the Southland Torcher could well be female." He added with a smirk, "Or it could be a 'they.'"

Norice said, more to herself it seemed, "I wonder what makes a person do such an awful thing."

Her comment was not lost on Clarissa, who prompted, "Different reasons trigger such behavior. A need to be noticed and become famous, getting a kick out of the sight of flames, dare to outsmart the authorities, or an outlet to vent ongoing anger. All of it is sick, of course, and in many cases, it is a cry for help."

She continued, "It's a fact that a majority of children are fascinated by fire and play with matches at one time or another, but they soon outgrow the urge. In a small percentage of adults that urge comes back, set off by emotional distress, and turns into an addiction."

Enzo changed the subject and addressed her with, "So you're a therapist. What's the difference between a therapist, a psychologist, or a psychiatrist?"

She smiled and replied, "Do you want it in a nutshell or a more detailed description?"

"Nutshell will do."

"Psychologists help patients handle stressful events, such as traumatic experiences, a family death, or long-term anxiety. They must earn a master's degree and a doctorate in psychology. Psychiatrists basically do the same thing plus diagnose mental disorders, focusing on chemical imbalances in the brain. The main difference between a psychologist and a psychiatrist is that psychologists are not medical doctors. They do not have a medical degree and are not trained in general medicine, nor can they prescribe medications. Psychiatrists, on the other hand, are medical physicians and must complete a four-year residency in psychiatry.

"As for therapists, they provide mental health services. To become a therapist in California, one must complete a master's or doctoral degree in psychology and accumulate supervised clinical experience of about 3000 hours and pass the California licensing exam. There are different types of therapy, such as play therapy, cognitive behavioral therapy, animal-assisted therapy, dialectal behavioral therapy, and many others."

Enzo thanked her and added, "I wonder what a detailed description would have amounted to."

Marvel thought, they may have a different approach, but all three are shrinks. In his view, most people who pursued a career in that line had mental issues of their own. However, he was careful not to voice his opinion aloud.

Mai turned toward Jaqueline seated next to her and asked, "And what does a social worker do?"

"It's an extremely broad field," replied Jaqueline. "There are psychiatric social workers who help people with mental illness; protective services social workers, supporting children, adults, and families who are at risk of harm; social hospital workers, and many more specialized branches of the job."

She continued, "I, for example, have two separate lines of duties. I work with pregnant teens, their boyfriends and parents by mentoring them. We social workers have a code of ethics, which means giving options to our charges but not telling them what to do. It is helpful to form groups for parents of the pregnant teen, teaching them how to set boundaries with kids and grandparents and deal with their frustrations. My other calling is as a hospice social worker, meaning that I deal with patients that are dying and their families."

She ended with, "The most important part of the job is confidentiality. We have a lot of compassion for the people we deal with but are not allowed to have a personal relationship. This is hard but necessary. If a social worker gets emotionally involved with the person she is helping, the danger of losing perspective is unavoidable. As to education, in order to become a certified social worker you must earn a Master's degree in social work."

This time Marvel spoke aloud and joked, "Someone better not ask me what a chiropractor does, or we'll be sitting here all day!"

There had been instant chemistry between Marvel and Clarissa from the moment they had introduced themselves to the group. So before the therapist could help it, she said, "I'll keep you in mind next time my back goes out."

Fed and full of energy, the guests moved on in pairs or single, ready to explore what Lake Castaic had to offer.

Hien Bong had not uttered another word since he'd introduced himself and his spouse 40 minutes earlier. Mai threw him an anxious glance as they left the room. He seemed in a world of his own, not paying attention to his surroundings. He was overworked, of course, but was there a more serious reason, she wondered. She worried about his mental health and hoped a week of relaxation by the lake would make him snap out of his depression.

CHAPTER 5

The guests purchased a week's pass to the State Park and by mid-morning were ready for adventure. Marvel headed to the fishing pier. The newlyweds took off on foot to explore the upper and lower lake. The Castelli brothers decided to head over to the boat rental place and look into jet skiing. Hien and Mai Bong drove their car to the swimming beach at the lower lake lagoon, which was also Jaqueline and Clarissa's choice, but the two ladies got a ride in their host's golf cart. Tim took off on his bicycle, playing his destinations by ear.

Jaqueline and Clarissa came out of the water after a swim in the pleasantly warm lake. They had spread out their blanket earlier close to the lifeguard booth and were eating their picnic lunch when Jaqueline said, "I didn't like that you mentioned my divorce to the group. Why did you?"

Clarissa replied, "We are going to be around these people for an entire week and I didn't want them to guess what our relationship is, so I thought it wouldn't hurt to make it clear that we are just friends. But my most important reason was to make it final to you that your life with your ex is over. I don't think that has sunk in completely."

Jaqueline kept quiet but knew that her friend was right.

"And another thing, stop taking your job home with you."

Again, there was silence between them but the remark was justified.

They were watching a couple of kayaking boats glide by when Clarissa suddenly announced, "Of course! Roland Pfadfinder!"

"What on earth are you talking about?"

"The owner of The Vista. I knew that he was no stranger to me but couldn't place him. Now I know. Sure, he changed his name, grew a beard, and wears glasses now, but he's none other than Roland Pfadfinder."

"The former newscaster?"

"The same," said Clarissa.

"Are you sure? I didn't scrutinize him closely, but Mr. Rhymes doesn't look like Pfadfinder in my opinion."

"His voice gives him away. I'm not mistaken."

"He must have legally changed his name then, in order to obtain the required permits to operate a bed and breakfast."

Clarissa stated, "Naturally, he did. He needed a business license, a food service license, and God knows what else."

"Well, I always liked him," remarked her friend.

"Sure, me too. But you cannot make up stuff as you report the news."

A distance away from the two ladies, the Bongs ate their lunch under the shade of a coast live oak tree.

Mai said, "It's peaceful here."

As there was no comment from Hien, she continued, "I sure hope you can relax this week and enjoy our little getaway. How about a short hike tomorrow? If your leg is acting up, making use of the trekking poles in the shed might be a good idea."

Again, there was no response.

The silence between them bothered Mai but didn't seem to have an impact on her spouse. She looked over to where the two women lay on their blanket, basking in the sun, and burst out, "I was impressed with the therapist lady at breakfast. She seems nice, maybe you should seek help from her."

"No! There is nothing wrong with me. I'm just tired. And don't you dare set something up. I forbid it."

They may have adjusted to American life and spoke fluent English, but their deep-rooted belief that the male was in charge made her not pursue the subject further. She swallowed her last bite, then stretched out and closed her eyes, trying to enjoy the peace around her.

CHAPTER 6

The honeymooners first backpacked along the Upper Castaic Lake trails, enjoying the spectacular view. A horseback rider and a couple of teens on their mountain bikes passed them, but they did not encounter any other hikers. Around noon they crossed over by the 425-foot Castaic Dam, then ate their lunch at one of the many picnic areas with a view to the lake at the lower lagoon.

Asher teased, "Having breakfast with all those people wasn't so bad. Right?"

"It was okay," Norice agreed, "But you have to admit that they're a weird group."

"How do you mean?"

"Oh, just an observation. For instance, I thought it odd that the teacher referred to his sibling as 'baby brother' when they're both middle-aged. The two women friends seem to be enthusiastic about their jobs, but the social worker - - I forgot her name - - is a nervous wreck. She kept twisting her napkin as if she were ready to strangle someone with it. The Asian couple didn't contribute to the conversation, either out of shyness or they have something to hide. "

She continued, "I like Marvel. He's funny, and it makes sense that he's here by himself, extending his stay after the convention. But I find it strange that Tim is alone. My instinct tells me there is something fishy about the guy. Who comes to a place like The Vista without a buddy?"

"Could be that he's a loner or that he can't find anyone to share his interest in bicycling."

"Maybe, but he has a shady eye."

Asher kidded, "I think you're around too many criminals in your job."

"Don't remind me of my job. I'm trying to forget about it this week."

He knew that she was in danger of burning out as a court reporter after only five years. True, the job was stressful, having to deal with gruesome subject matters, deadlines, let alone quarreling lawyers. But she was good at it and he would hate to see her quit.

Moving away from the sensitive subject, he said, "Are you in charge of all thank-you notes or do I need to chip in?"

She stared at him, uncomprehending.

"The mountain of wedding presents need to be addressed."

"Oh! I haven't given it a thought yet. Let's enjoy our week here first and worry about it later."

That settled, they left the picnic area and continued exploring the lower lake region, which had a lot more to offer.

CHAPTER 7

Marvel Maxwell was trying his luck for a nice catch from a fishing pier at the upper lake. He could not see the jet skiers but heard the noise from their motors even a long distance away. He shook his head and thought, I wonder if the bass can hear the racket and are spooked. That would account for them not biting. Oh well, I'm here for the fun of it and not because I need any catch on the table.

He packed up his fishing gear and looked for a perfect spot to eat his sandwich. Seated on a bench overlooking the lake, he enjoyed his food while thinking back to the conversations at breakfast. Talking about the Southland Torcher seems to be the Southern Californians' favorite topic these days, he mused. Then he smiled to himself, thinking, I'd have never imagined being attracted to a shrink, but I sure like that red-haired therapist. The name Clarissa Clever has a nice ring to it, and I bet she's clever to boot.

Sated by the picnic lunch The Vista's housekeeper had provided, he strolled back to the fishing pier but did not expect miracles. He planned to hike to the lower lake tomorrow and try his luck at float-tube fishing. Who knew, he might catch a heap of rainbow trout there.

The Castelli brothers, guilty of the noise that scared the fish away, were having the time of their lives on their jet ski. Both being beginners, they shared a personal watercraft rather than each riding their own. At the boat rental place they were instructed on how to operate the vehicle, including safety rules, and were informed of boating laws and regulations. Then they donned their life vests, plopped themselves onto the craft, and off they went.

Vigo sat in front and operated the controls while Enzo brought up the rear. Handling the jet ski was relatively easy to learn and Vigo soon became daring, increased the speed, and took sharp curves.

His brother held on to him and yelled above the noise of the motor, "It's like riding a snowmobile on water, only more thrilling and exhilarating!"

In the afternoon they rented a sailboat and enjoyed navigating on the lake at a slower pace. They had just returned the vessel to the rental place when Ralph drove up on his golf cart and offered to show them more lake attractions. They hopped on board and were taken on a sightseeing tour around the lower lake lagoon.

At the end of the day, Vigo said, "How about canoeing, kayaking, or maybe even waterskiing tomorrow?"

Enzo replied, "Let's do that later on in the week. I'd like to slow down tomorrow and do a bit of hiking, making use of the trekking poles in the shed that are available to us."

"Whatever keeps you happy," replied his brother.

"And at the same time I'll tend to my hobby."

"What hobby?"

"Caterpillars, of course."

"So you're still doing that?"

"Sure thing, they are fascinating creatures."

He went into a long speech of how rewarding the study of the species was.

Vigo had heard it before and paid little attention as Enzo continued, "Caterpillars can be discovered from early spring to early fall. The transition from caterpillar to butterfly takes about three weeks, with a week in the cocoon before emerging. When Ralph Rhymes drove us around, I spotted California sagebrush bushes at the lower lake and want to check them out."

"Check them out how?"

"For caterpillars, of course. They love those bushes. I packed my magnifier, just in case, and now I'm glad I did. If luck has it, I'll find some cocoons, and I'd be ecstatic if I saw the birth of a butterfly."

Vigo stated, "There is no way you can get me interested in searching for insects."

"They're not insects, and I don't expect you to come along."

"Okay then," said his brother, "we'll go our separate ways tomorrow. I may do some fishing while you chase butterflies."

CHAPTER 8

Tim had spent most of Tuesday exploring both the upper and lower lake, riding his bicycle all over the vast Castaic Lake area. Leaving the main roads around the shore behind and riding into the more remote areas, he got a sense of tranquility as he enjoyed nature. Still, he could not get the angry image of Amanda, his girlfriend, off his mind, as he had left their apartment Monday, slamming the door shut behind him.

Like always, their fight had been about the same issue they'd quarreled over for months. She had decided to go through with her foreign exchange program, sponsored by UCLA, to spend her senior year at a university in Pisa, Italy. He had tried to talk her out of it ever since she had mentioned her plan over a year ago, to no avail. And now, at the end of next month, she would hop on a plane to Europe and be gone for an entire year.

They had been dating ever since his sophomore year when she was a freshman and had started living together almost two years ago. To her, spending an entire year apart seemed to be no big deal and according to her, they would pick up where they'd left off upon her return. He, on the other hand, did not believe in long-distance relationships and had a tough time dealing with the idea.

As far as he was concerned, Amanda was the perfect woman for him, and he'd thought that she felt he was her guy. Now he had doubts about her true frame of mind. Clearly he was not one of her priorities.

Sure, she was majoring in foreign languages and literature. Her ultimate goal was to become a translator at the United Nations. Getting more fluent in the Italian language was her motivation, but she could easily do more intensive studying of that right here in Southern California. No, she was craving new adventures in Europe and her commitment to him came secondary.

That last thought made Tim angry all over again and he pedaled harder, to the point of working up a sweat.

CHAPTER 9

After clearing away the breakfast dishes and helping Kate put the kitchen back in order, Martina Padilla made sure all guests had left for the day before tending to their rooms. While making beds, dusting and vacuuming, she hummed a little tune to herself.

Martina was grateful for having been hired as housekeeper at The Vista, making it her hideout place. In order to get away from her domineering and controlling ex-fiancé, who could burst out into unprovoked rages at any time, she had to disappear without leaving a trace. After breaking off the engagement she swore to herself that she had endured the last beating ever. In order for the brute to be unable to find her, she had had no choice but to cut all ties to her former life. Upon taking the job here, she had texted her sister only one time, letting her know that she was okay but with a warning not to try to find her. After that, she cut off all communication. It was safer that way for all concerned, even though she felt lonely every so often.

Her employers were extremely understanding. Mrs. Rhymes even mentioned that in a way she and her husband were also hiding out. Martina had no idea what that meant but was smart enough not to question the remark.

Now, as she was taking care of their rooms, she amused herself by analyzing each guest. One can tell a lot about a person by the state of their space. For instance, she found the quarters of the brothers interesting. One was a slob, leaving his dirty clothes on the floor and his possessions scattered in disarray on his side of the room. The other was a neat freak. Everything was tucked away in either his suitcase, the closet, or dresser drawers. He had even made his own twin bed.

The African American man had stacks of brochures, gadgets, and free samples on his desk, among them a chiropractic adjusting tool. Obviously, it was stuff he had gathered while attending his convention. One look into his wardrobe indicated that he was a sharp dresser. She had noticed it all before since he'd occupied the room already over the past weekend.

The Asian couple's room was tidy. Either they were both neat or one picked up after the other. Their garments all hung in the closet, and their shoes were aligned on the shoe rack in perfect order. Even their pickleball paddles faced the same way.

The double sinks in the bathroom of the two female guests were indicators of their personalities. In addition to the toothbrush and hairbrush, one side was piled with cosmetics, like base makeup, coverup, day cream, night cream, mascara, and eye liner, as well as stuff Martina was unfamiliar with. The other side held only an electric toothbrush, sunscreen, and a hairbrush. She spotted a red hair in the hairbrush, so it must belong to the therapist lady, she deduced. Was she a "natural" who did not bother with makeup while here, wondered the housekeeper.

Martina giggled as she made the queen-size bed of the honeymooners. A bright-red sexy satin lace chemise nightie hung over one post of the bed and a pair of men's pajama shorts, also red, was flung over another.

Except for the unmade bed, Tim's room did not look occupied. The wardrobe and dresser stood empty. In the bathroom, a used towel and washcloth was the only sign that someone had showered. She remembered having seen the young man pedaling away on his bike wearing a backpack. So he must spend the day carrying all his possessions with him.

Well, she thought, that is one person who can leave the place at a moment's notice.

CHAPTER 10

As the Rhymes watched the evening news on TV, where the authorities dealt with another car chase all over the Southland, Ralph suddenly burst out, "What a boring newscaster. I could make the story far more interesting."

Sure you could, thought Kate. She imagined that, if he were in the newscaster's shoes, he'd claim to be in the pursuit vehicle himself, helping the police apprehend the culprit. Making stories more interesting was exactly what had got him fired. She knew better than to voice her opinion aloud, however.

Later, assuming to have his attention, she said, "I did some bookkeeping today. We are doing well, and if the full occupancy lasts for the entire summer and fall, we'll show a nice profit at the end of the year."

"Good," he said, but she could tell that his mind was elsewhere.

As to what went on in Ralph's head, he had a tough time dealing with his demons. On the surface it looked like he was adjusting to their new life out here in the boonies, but he could not help hating his situation. Was he doomed to spend the rest of his life chauffeuring guests around in a golf cart, making small talk? No wonder he resorted to his little secret hobby. The therapist woman would no doubt call it a cry for help.

He continued to muse, increasingly irritated with Kate's chipper enthusiasm. Was she really all that happy with their situation, or did she put up a good front? He could no longer tell. The woman whom he had pledged to share his life with seemed like a stranger to him these days. All she dwelled on was The Vista and what a unique and profitable establishment it was becoming. How she was striving to make it even better, blah, blah, blah. She didn't even miss their friends from a previous life, let alone care that his former colleagues and buddies avoided him now as if he had a deadly virus.

When the news was over, Kate tuned in to one of her favorite TV shows, while Ralph went to his study and turned on the computer.

CHAPTER 11

On Tuesday evening, the Castelli brothers headed over to a sports bar eatery in nearby Saugus. They plopped onto barstools and ordered pulled pork sandwiches and beer. It was too early for the place to be crowded. Except for a lonely man at the other end of the bar, they had the space to themselves. They ate in silence, watching the LA Dodgers on the big screen TV, where Major League Baseball was happening.

Sated and on their second beer, they motioned to the bartender to turn the TV volume down. With the sound of the game in progress muffled, it was easier for them to have a conversation.

Vigo said, "I haven't always been a good older brother to you, but I'm glad we're spending this week together before you leave for Texas."

"Me too. I appreciate you taking the time and that Rachel is okay with it. You have a great wife," replied Enzo.

"Thanks, but no big deal. As a teacher I'm free as a bird all summer, and Rachel takes the girls for a visit to her folks in Vancouver, Canada, at least once a year, so decided she may as well do so now."

"I envy you. You have a great wife and two wonderful kids." As an afterthought he added, "And what do I have to show for myself? A couple of failed marriages and no descendants."

"Now, don't feel sorry for yourself. You had some bad luck but you also have mostly yourself to blame for your situation. Your gambling problem made you become a different person, but I'm relieved to know that you left it all behind."

Enzo stated, "It wasn't just a problem but a full-blown addiction. I'm over and done with it, but I'll stay away from casinos for the rest of my life, just in case."

"Glad to hear it," said Vigo. "As to my own idyllic life, Rachel and I have had our ups and downs. In fact, we disagree right now."

"Really?"

Vigo made light of it and said, "You don't want to know, it's too ridiculous. We're basically fighting over politics."

He looked up at the big screen above their heads and said, "Damn, we just missed a home run!"

Their eyes were glued to the TV for a while, watching the Dodger fans cheering. The happy screams of the crowd were contagious as the brothers joined in with their own cheers.

Enzo remarked, "California is a great place, after all."

"You're not having cold feet about moving away, or are you?"

"Oh no, I'm planning to have a fresh clean slate in Texas, professionally and otherwise. And this time I won't screw up."

"Atta boy!"

Meanwhile, Marvel had invited Jaqueline and Clarissa to dinner at a local restaurant. Marvel was entertaining as he educated them about his chiropractor practice. Some of his anecdotes were hilarious, making both women burst out laughing, until they got looks from people seated at the next table. But in the end, he got serious and, handing Clarissa his business card, said, "I'll be happy to treat you next time your back goes out."

"I'll keep that in mind," she replied, and tucked the card into her purse.

Back at The Vista and in their room, Jaqueline said, "You like him, right?"

Nodding, Clarissa replied, "Is it that obvious?"

CHAPTER 12

When Tim woke up on Wednesday, he had a change of heart. No longer angry at Amanda, only saddened that they'd be apart soon, he decided to ride home a day earlier than planned and make peace. He would no longer try to persuade her to cancel her plans but would make an effort to be especially nice in the time they had left together. This way he hoped that she would think kindly of him during her year away.

He found Mrs. Rhymes already in her office at 7:15 in the morning and said, "I'm leaving today instead of tomorrow and hope that's not a problem."

She replied, "It's not, but I hope you don't have an issue with your accommodation at The Vista. If so, what can I do to make you more comfortable?"

"No issue at all. I just woke up feeling homesick."

She winked and remarked, "Miss your girlfriend already, hmm?"

He nodded.

"Since you've prepaid, I'll credit you for today. Stay for breakfast, though. It's included in yesterday's lodging."

"Thanks, I will," he said, and went back to his room.

Kate smiled and thought, there's nothing sweeter than young love. It wasn't all that long ago since Roland had been her own young lover. Secretly and to herself, she still thought of him as Roland.

She sighed and checked her watch. It was time to head over to the kitchen to help Martina prepare breakfast.

CHAPTER 13

Things did not go harmoniously in Jaqueline and Clarissa's room that morning. While the former was in the shower, Clarissa lingered in bed, trying not to resent her friend. Funny how one did not truly know a person until spending time under the same roof. It was the second night that she had lost sleep due to Jaqueline's weird habit. On the first night she'd kept quiet and shrugged it off as the other's adjustment to new surroundings and a strange bed. Not so this past night.

When her friend turned on the light at two o'clock again, sat up in her twin bed and started reading a book, Clarissa hissed, "Turn off the light!"

"Oh, you're awake?"

"Yes, and I was last night too. I'm not going to lose sleep again, so turn it off."

Jacqueline did as told but tossed and turned, went to the bathroom twice without taking care to do it quietly, making it miserable for both for the remainder of the night.

When Jaqueline came back from her shower, Clarissa decided to clear the air and asked, "So how long has this reading in bed in the middle of the night been going on?"

"A few months," the other replied reluctantly, "but I only read for about half an hour, then try to go back to sleep."

"Well, stop. It's unhealthy behavior. Count sheep, count backwards from 100, or take a sleeping pill, if you have to."

As Jaqueline turned around and went back into the bathroom, Clarissa sighed and thought, now she's pouting and hogs the place for an eternity and I have to pee. Why put on mascara and stuff when we're just going to swim in the lake? Her ex-husband is a jerk. Still, I'm starting to see that she's not an easy person to live with.

By the time the two women showed up for breakfast, they were okay with one another again and looked forward to a new day of relaxation.

CHAPTER 14

Marvel Maxwell woke up to another day of leisure. He was determined to have a relaxed time during his stay at The Vista and not worry about what awaited him at home. The truth was that he would have to face a malpractice lawsuit. Attending the convention had been a welcomed distraction and prolonging his absence from home by staying near Lake Castaic was another diversion, but he could not help being anxious about what lay ahead.

The malpractice suit was unfounded, but one never knew what a jury would decide. He had only testified in court one time when he was subpoenaed by the prosecution as a witness in a criminal case. The defense attorney had twisted his words around to the point of him no longer being sure what he had seen.

Now he would be the defendant and he assumed that the prosecutor would use similar tricks and try to prove that negligence played a role in the treatment of his patient. The attorney would argue that by manipulation of the patient's neck, arteries to the brain became ruptured and therefore claim that the treatment caused a stroke.

Marvel was shaving as he thought, there was nothing wrong with the treatment I performed. Judging by the information I had to work with, there was no negligence on my part. The patient was not truthful about the medications he was taking, nor that he had had a previous stroke. Had I known about these factors; I would have resorted to a different treatment. Sure, I have medical malpractice insurance, but the point is that I did nothing wrong.

"Ouch!" he cried out, as he nicked himself with the razor blade.

Then he laughed at the reflection that stared back at him from the mirror and decided not to let worry over the malpractice suit ruin the float-tube fishing he was planning for the day.

CHAPTER 15

By Wednesday morning, Mai Bong had made up her mind to get help for her husband's state of mind. The clincher was when she had suggested that they take advantage of the pickleball court a few minutes' drive away and he claimed not to feel like playing. "Not to feel like playing!" she had repeated. "It's your favorite pastime." To which he had just shrugged his shoulders.

Forget traditional obedience to the male spouse, she told herself. Then she confronted Hien with, "Even without your approval, I'm going to talk with Clarissa at breakfast and set up an appointment."

"You do what you want but count me out. I'm staying in our room."

An hour later, to Mai's disappointment, Martina, the housekeeper, had carried a tray of food to him after she had told everyone at breakfast that her husband was not feeling well.

That does it, Mai thought. He can stay put and feel sorry for himself all day, but I'm going out exploring alone and won't feel guilty in the least. And she congratulated herself when she had the courage to put that thought into action.

After breakfast, all guests stuck to their agenda for the day. The honeymooners, Asher and Norice, drove over to Magic Mountain for a day of thrilling rides at the amusement park. Tim set out for more exploration on his bicycle around the lake and beyond before planning to head home in the afternoon. And the rest followed up on plans they had made the day before.

Kate needed to run errands and do a week's grocery shopping, while Ralph stayed behind, ready to chauffeur the guests on his golf cart and assist them as needed. After making up the lodgers' rooms, Martina had the afternoon free and looked forward to watching a movie on Netflix.

The arsonist had a different agenda.

CHAPTER 16

Near noon, with the sun at its strongest, the so-called Southland Torcher slowly climbed up a slope leading away from the lower lake and, getting to the top of the slight hill, glanced back to make sure no one was in sight. Descending a few yards down the opposite side of the mound, the person arrived at a remote spot with no walkways or trails on that side leading to the immediate area, but there was an abundance of dried grass and brush.

The arsonist reflected on how he'd arrived at the obsession. It all started with the discovery of a unique way to set off a fire. After the initial satisfaction of proving that the method worked, the person discovered the thrill of watching the blaze, and so it became an addiction. Said method left no trace behind, making it the main reason the authorities had not caught on to date.

Following that first fire, the individual had tried hard to overcome their fascination with flames to no avail and wondered whether becoming a firefighter would have done the trick. Fighting fires instead of setting them might have satisfied the need to be around them. Too late to envision that now. The perpetrator never meant for anybody to get killed but it happened. So it had to stop.

On this day at the Lake Castaic area, the arsonist made a resolution that this would be the very last time they gave in to the ravaging impulse.

Getting down to the business at hand, *One for the road, then quit for good*, was the Southland Torcher's motto.

"What the hell are you doing!" came a shout from on top of the hill.

The arsonist tried to undo what was set into motion, but it was too late. The dried-up brush from months of drought had already burst into flames. The torcher hollered back, "I don't know how that happened but let's get out of here and call the authorities."

CHAPTER 17

Minutes later, a man on horseback noticed smoke coming from behind that hill and called 911. Another several minutes had passed when Ralph saw the smoke while driving his golf cart in the vicinity of the lower lake, but by that time he could also hear the sirens of the fire engines and, seconds later, saw numerous fire trucks making their way into the State Park.

He tried to reach all guests who were scattered all over the lower lake, informing them of the possible danger and asking everyone to hurry around to the upper lake and meet at The Vista. He was hoping that there would be no evacuation order, but if so, it would be easier if they gathered at "home base."

Clarissa and Jaqueline were laying out at the swim beach and had been unaware of the fire before Ralph hit them with the news and offered them a ride home. They found Vigo at the fishing pier and asked him to hop on board. Marvel was float-tube fishing out on the lake and seemed to have no care in the world. Spotting him, Ralph blew his emergency whistle, which could be heard for half a mile away. It not only got Marvel's attention but also that of other people who were enjoying recreation on the lake. Ralph pointed in the direction where the fire engines were headed. That, plus the rising smoke coming from somewhere behind the south of the lake, made them aware that all was not well.

Ralph and his passengers encountered Enzo on a trail parallel to the road, frantically using trekking poles and marching north at a steady pace, no doubt aware of the fire.

Ralph shouted, "Meet you at The Vista!"

Enzo nodded and marched on.

A few yards farther, they found Hien sitting on the rocky ground close by the shore, staring into the lake, oblivious to his surroundings.

Ralph shouted to get his attention, ordering him to hop on the golf cart, where the two ladies squeezed together on the back seat to make room. Hien came on board but was in no hurry. Even as Clarissa pointed at the smoke rising to the sky a distance away and a helicopter dropping water onto the flames, the fact that they could be in danger did not seem to register with Hien.

When they were close to home, Mai passed them in a car coming from the opposite direction, looking for Hien.

Seeing her husband out of harm's way, she rolled down her window and yelled, "I've been looking all over for you. Thank God you are safe!"

After arriving at The Vista, Ralph sighed with relief. As far as he knew, Tim had checked out that morning and was most likely home by now. The newlyweds had spent the day at Magic Mountain, so all guests were accounted for. He found Kate and the housekeeper safe and sound in the kitchen and was thankful for it.

CHAPTER 18

In the early evening, the Rhymes asked all guests and Martina to gather in the dining room.

Kate took the initiative and said, "In case you haven't heard the news, as of right now, the brushfire has been surrounded and is 98% contained. Thanks to the person on horseback, who reported the fire to the authorities soon after it started, the firefighters came on the scene promptly and were able to stop the flames before they got out of hand and reached structures. There is no longer any danger to the Castaic Lake community."

"Thank God. What a scare!" said Mai. And she added, "Could the fire have been set by the Southland Torcher?"

"No doubt that's a strong possibility," said Clarissa.

Marvel turned to the Jenkinses, who had returned from Magic Mountain minutes earlier, and remarked, "You've missed all the excitement."

"And so has Tim," Jaqueline said.

Mai shook her head and stated, "I saw him bicycling near the lower lake a short time before noon. He must have left around the time the fire broke out."

Norice put into words what most were thinking, by saying, "How convenient!"

"What do you mean?" someone asked.

"Isn't it obvious?"

At that moment Kate's cell phone chimed. As she answered it, the rest of the assembled heard the one-sided conversation.

"Yes, speaking."

"No. Not as far as I know."

"I see."

"Of course. Give it to me."

After ending the call and jotting a number into her contact list, Kate stated, "Speaking of the devil, that was Tim's girlfriend, wanting to know if Tim was still here. According to her, she had received a text from him minutes before noon with the message that he was leaving Castaic and would be home around three o'clock. He has not shown up at their home yet, and when the woman contacted the police, she was told that no bicycler accident had been reported."

Asher asked, to no one in particular, "Do you think he's still here?"

Ralph answered, "I doubt that. The room he occupied no longer holds his belongings. He must have changed his mind about going home. Where he headed instead is anyone's guess."

Martina spoke up, saying, "He always took his belongings with him. His room was empty after he left on Tuesday too."

Norice said, "It doesn't matter where he went, but he conveniently is getting lost and therefore avoiding being questioned by the authorities, is my opinion. I'm sure we all agree that he must be none other than the Southland Torcher."

"Hold on," objected Marvel, "let's not jump to conclusions. You as a court reporter, of all people, should know better than to accuse someone without due process."

"I agree," Vigo chimed in, while his brother nodded.

All guests were in a somber mood as they ambled out of the room and made dinner plans.

On the evening news the fire chief made an appearance and stated that the brush fire at Castaic Lake was 100% contained;. that no flare-ups had been detected, neither by the ground crew nor the low-flying planes; and thanks to the great efforts of his firefighters, the near wind-still conditions, and the favorable terrain, he was happy to report that no damage to buildings and no harm to people took place.

When asked by a reporter whether the blaze had been the work of an arsonist, the fire chief replied, "As to that, it is too early for me to form an opinion. We are launching an investigation."

CHAPTER 19

Tim's girlfriend, Amanda Redding, spent a sleepless night from Wednesday to Thursday. Yes, she had been furious at Tim when he'd left on Monday. She could not understand that a man in this day and age could be so possessive as not to realize how important broadening her horizon was to her.

But then, he had sent her that endearing text and not only did she forgive him but couldn't wait to see him. She had read the text numerous times, and lying awake now remembered it word for word:

Please forgive me, Amanda. I am such a fool. How can I keep you from following your dream? I can see now that it is out of selfishness that I want you here. I'll try my best to only look at the positive aspects of your studies abroad. After all, what is one year compared to the rest of our lives? As to right now, I miss you already and plan to cut my stay here by one day. I'm about to leave Castaic Lake now and should be home no later than three o'clock.

Love you, Tim

So what had happened to him after he'd sent that text? According to the police, he had not been in an accident. The woman owner of The Vista claimed he was no longer there. Naturally, Amanda had called his cellphone numerous times after she'd expected him home at three. Each time it went to voicemail.

On the evening news she had learned of the brush fire at Castaic Lake. Her worries that he might have been caught in the blaze were soon dismissed when she also learned that the fire had already been contained and that there were no structural losses, fatalities or injured persons.

So where the hell was he, she wondered . He would not have changed his mind about coming home without letting her know. She was sure of that. And if he'd had a flat tire or some other mishap along the way, he would have called or texted.

Amanda finally dozed off into a restless sleep at 3:00 a.m. but not before resolving to drive to Lake Castaic in the morning and trace Tim's whereabouts from where he had sent her that text.

CHAPTER 20

At seven o'clock Thursday morning Kate stuck her head into the bathroom door where Ralph had finished showering and was in the process of brushing his teeth.

She said, "Tim Weinbau's girlfriend called again and informed me that she's on her way here."

"Why?"

"Tim still isn't home, nor has she heard from him, and she insists that something must have happened to him. She wants to trace his whereabouts, is how she put it."

Ralph spat out the toothpaste and said, "Does the woman think we're hiding Tim here, or something?"

"Maybe. Who knows? By the way, the woman's name is Amanda Redding. She sounds determined and wants to book a room in case she decides to stay overnight. I'm giving her the room Tim vacated. Martina already changed the sheets and prepared it for a new guest."

Before starting to floss, Ralph stated, "What does she need to snoop around here for? The guy left yesterday and it's none of our business where he went from here. Has it even occurred to her that maybe he wants to ditch her but doesn't have the balls to tell her and face the music?"

"You have a point, but she sounded really worried and seems to think that something happened to him."

"Well, nobody perished in the fire. That's a fact. And I'm starting to agree with some of the guests that he may well be the Southland Torcher and skipped town in order not to be interrogated."

Kate said, "If he is the arsonist, running away would draw suspicion to him. The smart thing would be to ride home and act innocent. Don't you think?"

"I don't know what to think anymore," replied her husband, "but it's a fact that he is no longer here."

CHAPTER 21

The guests were enjoying their breakfast when Kate burst into the room with a young woman in tow.

She said, "This is Amanda Redding, Tim Weinbau's girlfriend. She has some questions, so please cooperate." And turning to Amanda, she asked, "What would you like for breakfast?"

"Nothing, thanks. I'm not hungry," Amanda replied, and sat down at one end of the table where there was an empty seat which previously had been Tim's spot.

As The Vista's owner left the dining room, everyone became tongue-tied, not sure what to expect. A couple of guests resorted to a muffled greeting, but most appeared to be suddenly preoccupied with their food.

Amanda broke the silence, saying, "Tim and I live together and he hasn't come home. I talked with the police and reported him missing. They assured me that no accident involving a bicyclist was recorded. And they made it clear that the police won't interfere if an adult is missing when there is no reason to believe that the person is in immediate harm's way."

She went on, "Since the authorities are no help to me, I'm looking for him on my own. I started off at the crack of dawn this morning, taking surface streets all the way over here, making sure that there was no trace of Tim along the way."

She fixed each person with a steady gaze from her green eyes as she continued, "You do understand that I need to start here, where he was last seen."

All the guests agreed that they had socialized with Tim at breakfast and that he seemed perfectly fine then. To Amanda's question about anyone having talked with him later in the morning, they either shook their heads or stayed silent.

Enzo said, "There is a simple explanation. Has it occurred to you that the young man just wants to disappear?"

She slapped her fist onto the table, making everyone jump, and stated, "That's not an option! He was planning to come home. I have a text from him to prove it."

The guests who believed Tim to be the Southland Torcher, responsible for the local blaze, judged it inappropriate to voice their opinion to his girlfriend. And the ones who tended to think that Tim may have gotten cold feet and wanted out of the relationship also kept that thought to themselves.

Marvel reflected that they were dealing with a forceful and determined young woman who would leave no stone unturned to get at the truth. Like the rest of his fellow guests, he kept the thought to himself.

As the silence in the room grew, Amanda pleaded, "If any of you talked with Tim yesterday, particularly close to noon, please let me know. You don't need to do so right now but come see me privately."

That said, she got up and, as she walked toward the door, turned her head in their direction and stated, "I'll be waiting in my guest room."

CHAPTER 22

Amanda knew that she was given the room that Tim had vacated the previous day. It was the only available one in the place. She decided to systematically check it for clues. Maybe he had left something behind that would lead her in the right direction. The closet and dresser were empty and so was the small desk. She checked behind each piece of furniture and crawled on her hands and knees to look underneath the bed. Everything was spotless and devoid of any clue. After lifting up the mattress and peeking below, she finally gave up the search. There was no trace of Tim in the room; even his scent was gone.

She pulled the only chair in the room up close to the window and looked out, allowing her a magnificent view of the tranquil upper lake. She was just thinking that tranquility was the farthest thing from her mind at the moment, when there was a knock at the door.

"Come on in!" she yelled.

Mai opened the door and hesitated for a second before stepping into the room and closing it gently behind her.

Amanda got up, offered her the chair, and plopping herself onto the edge of the bed, said, "Thanks for coming. So you talked to Tim yesterday?"

"We didn't speak. He didn't notice me, but I saw him. So I doubt this helps you," Mai replied.

"Everything helps! At what time and where did you see him?"

"I don't remember the time but it was before noon. I was on my way back to the bed and breakfast and - - -"

Amanda interrupted, "On foot?"

"No, by car. I drove back to The Vista to see if my husband was ready for lunch. I made a wrong turn and ended up on a 'no outlet' end of the road. It was when I turned the car around and headed back where I came from that I saw Tim on his bicycle. Like I said, he didn't notice me, but I saw him riding up a small hill."

Amanda had studied the map on the wall in the hallway and now wanted to know, "Where was this in proximity to the lake?"

"It was in a remote area of the lower lake where not much is going on. At least I didn't encounter anyone except for your boyfriend."

"Was it far away from the lake?"

"Oh, no," said Mai, "it was close to the lake but where there are no recreational activities."

"Can you show me exactly where, if we go there?"

Mai reflected and then said, "Sure. I'll try to find the exact place."

CHAPTER 23

They took the Bongs' car. Mai had asked Hien to come along, but he refused, insisting that Mai should not have gotten involved in the first place. "Nothing good will come from your meddling," he had warned.

Now, heading toward the lower lake, Mai had second thoughts. What if her husband was right? Nonsense, she told herself. There is nothing wrong with helping the young woman with her quest to learn the truth about her boyfriend's disappearance.

When they arrived at the isolated area where there was a fork in the road with one way continuing parallel with the lake, the other leading to a dead-end, Mai stopped the car.

She said, "It was here where I first drove the wrong way. Then, after I turned around and came back, I saw Tim."

She pointed a finger to a path that led up a small slope, stating, "He was riding up that little hill."

Amanda asked, "Are you sure this is where you saw him."

"I'm positive."

A helicopter flew overhead and after the noise from it faded, Mai remarked, "The fire was already completely contained yesterday, but they're still checking to make sure that there are no flare-ups."

Far from being distracted by the chopper, Amanda pointed toward the incline and said, "The pathway up the hill is obviously off limits to cars. I'll walk the short distance since I'm curious what it looks like down the other side. You may leave me now. Thanks so much for your help. I'll find my way back to the bed and breakfast on foot later."

Mai's first impulse was to say that she'd wait and give her a ride back, but Amanda had already stepped out of the car and started walking. It was clear that the young woman wanted to be alone for whatever mission she was on. So Mai shrugged her shoulders and drove away.

Before Amanda reached the top of the rise, there was evidence of the brush fire, but once she arrived, the devastation below her was immense. The blackened terrain of the brush reached as far as the eye could see and the few trees that were still standing were scorched. There had been loose-flying ashes all along the entire area, ever since she had arrived at Lake Castaic, but here there was a solid layer of them.

Kudos to the firefighters who had contained the blaze so quickly, she thought. Then her mind immediately switched back to her mission. So if Mai spoke the truth, and there is no reason why she wouldn't, Tim had ridden his bike up here shortly before noon yesterday. The time on the text he sent her was 11:45. On it he had stated that he was about to leave the Lake Castaic State Park and head home. So why didn't he?

She deduced that soon after that time a brush fire was spotted in this area. Even though the authorities had not mentioned the fact, it was obvious that the fire had been set by an arsonist, as it had not been windy, nor were there electrical lines anywhere nearby. And what's more, she suspected it to be the work of none other than the Southland Torcher.

There could only be two possibilities, she reflected. Either Tim was the culprit, or he had witnessed the torcher in action. She was 100% sure that Tim was innocent. So it must be that he had caught the arsonist in the act of setting the fire.

Her heart started beating uncontrollably with the realization that, if so, the torcher must have worried about being identified and therefore caught. There would not only be arson charges but also a murder charge for the Malibu fatality. This meant that Tim needed to be silenced. All the worry she had felt from the moment she had realized that Tim was missing, and leaving no stone unturned to find him, came to a crushing and devastating climax.

She suddenly started to shake, feeling weak and dizzy. Whether this was from lack of sleep and consuming only coffee and no food for breakfast or the shock that Tim may have been killed was irrelevant.

Take a deep breath, she told herself, you can't allow yourself to fall apart. You owe it to Tim to learn the truth.

CHAPTER 24

Amanda pulled herself together and decided to reconstruct what she thought must have happened. There was no point in advancing to the destruction. A stake had been erected a few feet away from where she stood with a sign which read: *Restricted area. Keep out!* And a bit farther down the slope, she noticed fire investigators at their job, going through debris and rubble left all over the burned area.

She dismissed the idea that the arsonist had struck Tim down, then pushed him into the burning brush. The firefighters on the ground or in the air would have found him long ago. She remembered the newscaster's announcement from the night before, word for word; *There were no fatalities or injured persons.*

So what had happened? Tim seemed to have vanished without a trace. She shook her head, turned around, then slowly trekked back down the hill, her heart racing. A sudden urge to see him made her reach for her phone in her jeans back pocket, as she meant to watch a video he had sent her weeks ago. Out of sheer habit, she dialed his number instead.

Was that the faint ringing of a phone she heard? Amanda stopped in her tracks. Aware that the sound was coming from among bushes below her, she rushed to the area and fumbled through the shrubs until she found the cellphone.

She picked it up and yelled aloud, "Oh my God!" as she realized that it was indeed Tim's phone. She didn't know his password so could not unlock it but was sure it was Tim's. It had a *Tour de France* protective case he had designed himself. The thing only had 7% battery life left, so Amanda had found it in the nick of time.

The young woman put her mind back to reconstruct mode. It was obvious that Tim had lost his phone or tossed it into the bushes on purpose soon after he sent her the text. But where did he go, or was forced to go, from here? she pondered. If he had witnessed the torcher's handiwork and was presumably on his bike, why not pedal away as fast as possible and call the authorities? There must have been a struggle where the arsonist overpowered him. But what could have taken place next?

She had already established that he did not perish in the fire. Was he forced at gunpoint or threatened with a knife to ride somewhere? That's stupid, she corrected herself as soon as the thought had entered her mind. The arsonist could not have foreseen being observed and would not have had a weapon at the ready. The idea that Tim was forced to ride out of the area also made no sense. The villain must have decided to deal with him right on the spot. But how? Was it possible that Tim could have been bribed? No way, she answered her own question. Her next thought was that it looked like Mai had been the last person to have seen her boyfriend before he vanished.

At this point of her musing, Amanda had arrived at the road leading around the lake. She stepped a few paces below it and walked toward the shoreline.

And there she saw them! They were faint, but she was not mistaken. There were *bicycle tracks* in the sand leading down to the lake. She followed them to where they stopped right at the water's edge.

She stared into the water, then walked along the shore, searching the area with her eyes never leaving the lake, but there was no trace of either the bike or Tim.

The worst of Amanda's nightmare had become a reality and she could no longer believe she would find Tim alive. She sat down on a rock at the water's edge and, when she stopped shaking, called 911.

CHAPTER 25

Amanda had the authorities convinced that her suspicions were justified. The finding of Tim's phone and the evidence of bicycle tracks leading into the water warranted an investigation.

On Friday morning, July 18, a team of divers searched the immediate area of the lower lake where Amanda had made her discoveries. All boating activities on that part of the lagoon were forbidden. By 11:00 a.m., the bicycle was discovered at the bottom of the lake, and it took a good part of the afternoon to haul it up and out of the water. Close to dusk, when the search was about to be postponed until the next day, one of the divers found the body a quarter mile downstream.

The corpse was caught among dead branches and other debris on a boulder close to the surface. Hauling it on shore proved to be relatively easy.

Law enforcement was called to the scene and soon afterwards the coroner drove up and did a quick primary examination of the corpse before it was carted off to the morgue.

When Amanda heard the news that Tim's body had been found, it was no longer a shock since in her mind she had known his fate as soon as she had discovered the two pieces of evidence. She would allow herself to mourn Tim later; all she could concentrate on now was to avenge him. So she bravely drove to the morgue to identify his body and thought she was prepared for an ugly sight.

Nothing could have prepared her, though, for what she saw when the sheet covering Tim was lifted. His entire body was bloated and what remained of the face was grotesque, but she nodded in the affirmative and then sprinted to the nearest sink to vomit.

CHAPTER 26

Sheriff Simon Shaft was in charge of the homicide investigation into Tim's death. There was no question of either accident or suicide. The idea that someone would ride their bicycle into a lake by accident was absurd, and doing so to commit suicide was an even less likely possibility. If a person wanted to end their life by drowning in this neighborhood, jumping into the water from the Castaic Dam would be more efficient.

Sheriff Shaft was 47 years old. He had a wife and two teenage kids whom he loved dearly, but he never let family life interfere with his professional duties. He was known for his unorthodox approach to cases, but since he was excellent at his job, the fact that he sometimes did not abide by protocol was overlooked.

The sheriff had had a brief consultation with the victim's girlfriend, Amanda Redding, on Friday evening after she had identified the body. Even obviously under stress, the young woman had gone over her discovery in a precise and competent manner. There was no doubt in his mind that she had a sharp intellect. After the meeting, he had done a background check on her. She was 21 and about to start her senior year of college. Everything else she had shared with him in her interview was the truth.

Before heading home on Friday evening, the sheriff studied the information he had so far about the homicide. It amounted to little indeed. He had briefly talked with the coroner on scene, who had put the time of death between 15 minutes before noon and 1:00 p.m. on Wednesday. Cause of death was drowning, which was hardly a surprise. The coroner had promised a rush order with the autopsy, and the sheriff hoped to get his report in due course.

Sheriff Shaft did not believe in coincidences. It stood to reason that the murder was a direct consequence of a witness having caught the arsonist setting the fire. Like the young woman had mentioned, "The victim was seen riding his bicycle toward where the fire had broken out moments later."

It also made sense that the Torcher was one of the guests currently staying at The Vista. A slight possibility was that the culprit could be a total stranger, but Sheriff Shaft had to go with the assumption that it was one of the bed and breakfast lodgers. Considering all the fires the Southland Torcher was responsible for and leaving no clue behind, here at long last there were plausible suspects.

It would not normally be his job to investigate arson,, but he could not help thinking that it would be a bonus to catch the Torcher along with Tim Weinbau's murderer.

As far as interrogating the suspects, he decided that, rather than having each person come to the station, he would go to The Vista and conduct his interrogation there. He sighed and thought, I'm scheduled to be on duty tomorrow, Saturday, but have a feeling that this case will make me work through the entire weekend and beyond. He knew that his wife would not be pleased since he had promised her an outing on Sunday, but she had learned long ago that unexpected duties came with the territory.

CHAPTER 27

Breakfast on Saturday morning was somber. The events of the previous two days had left everyone in a grave and pensive mood. Guests avoided eye contact with one another, aware that one of them might be an arsonist, and even worse, a killer. Kate and Martina had prepared a tasty meal of French toast, scrambled eggs and bacon, but most lodgers barely had an appetite and forced themselves to eat a few bites.

As Amanda entered the dining room, Norice whispered to Asher, "What do we say to someone whose boyfriend was murdered? 'Sorry for your loss' doesn't seem right."

"Nothing said is best," he mumbled back.

Toward the end of the meal, Kate announced that the sheriff was going to talk with each person privately in the recreation room. She said that she was sorry to inconvenience everyone but it was necessary that they all stayed at The Vista while waiting to be interviewed. Until it was each guest's turn, they could wait in their room or were welcome to stay in the dining room.

Marvel said, "Under the circumstances, I no longer have a desire to take advantage of what the lake and its surroundings have to offer and assume that everyone else here feels the same. In addition to the investigation of poor Tim's murder, nobody wants to deal with the unhealthy air quality outside. I was going to cut my stay short and leave today but don't mind sticking around for the interview with the sheriff."

Most guests either nodded in agreement or made similar statements. Nobody was pleased to be retained and questioned, but if they secretly dreaded it, they hid the fact in order not to look guilty.

CHAPTER 28

In the recreation room Kate had cleared the assorted games off a card table and placed two chairs facing each other across it. In a far corner of the room she had also set a small piece of furniture, no larger than a TV tray, and placed a folding chair by it.

Sheriff Shaft glanced over to where Amanda was seated in her niche and wondered how she had talked him into sitting in on the interviews. Initially, he had told her that he liked to work alone on a case and that he didn't see the benefit of a layperson joining him in the investigation. She countered that she would not interfere with his questioning but just sit quietly and observe. "I'm good at taking notes, so you don't have to bother with that," she had stated. And when he still hesitated, she had added, "Keep in mind, if it wasn't for me, you would not have a case to investigate, let alone finally catch the Southland Torcher."

He knew that she had a point. Also, from her demeanor during their talk the evening before and again this morning when she intercepted him as he stepped out of his car, it was clear that the young woman had her emotions under control. So he gave in but warned her that, should she show any attempt of meddling, she'd be out the door in a flash.

Now he couldn't help but chuckle to himself as she pulled a legal pad and pen for taking notes out of her large purse. Being of her generation, and a university student to boot, he would have expected some kind of an electronic device.

Having an excellent memory, he did not take notes as a rule but decided that in this case it would not hurt if Amanda took them. The only document he now placed before him was a list of the guests' names, their home addresses and phone numbers, and their occupations that Mrs. Rhymes had provided. It was also thanks to her that he had a map with all activities on the lake listed.

Before entering the recreation room he had studied the large map which hung on the wall in the hallway. She had informed him that it was the enlargement of the pocket size maps that the State Park provided upon request. "I keep some in my office," she had said, and promptly went to fetch him one.

Now Kate stepped into the room and said, "It's going to be a hot day," and placed a small bottle of water at easy reach for Sheriff Shaft and handed another to Amanda. Then she turned back to the law enforcer and asked, "Who shall I send in first?"

"Thanks, Mrs. Rhymes. Let's start with the people in your household. You first."

CHAPTER 29

That the sheriff included "the people in her household," as he put it, on his suspect list came as a shocking surprise to Kate. Still, she recovered fast, sat down in the chair facing him across the card table and, putting on her best poker face, said, "Yes, sir. I'm at your disposal."

Sheriff Shaft asked, "Describe your movements on Wednesday mid-morning, July 16, let's say from about 10:00 a.m. until noon."

She reflected for a moment and then stated, "I was running errands and left the house shortly after ten. First I stopped to get gas, then took care of some banking, and finally did a week's grocery shopping. I didn't look at the time when I came back but my guess is that it was after 11:30, probably closer to 12:00."

"What did you do upon returning to The Vista?"

She had a hard time not rolling her eyes as she said, "I unpacked a dozen bags of groceries and Martina helped me put everything away in the fridge and cabinets." She added, "I can show you the store receipt for proof."

"That won't be necessary," he replied with a smirk, then continued, "Where were you when you first became aware of the brush fire?"

"I was still in the kitchen, deciding what to fix for lunch, when I heard a helicopter. Then I looked out the window and saw smoke rising from somewhere in the lower lake area."

"Did you encounter anyone at that time?"

She replied, "Martina was still with me."

"I meant any of the guests."

"No. As far as I know, they were all enjoying outdoor activities. Oh, wait! I almost forgot. A bit later Mai Bong came into the kitchen, looking for her husband."

The sheriff posed one last question by asking, "By chance, did Tim Weinbau tell you his plans for Wednesday?"

Kate answered in the negative and added, "He checked out a day earlier than he had reserved, and I assumed that he left for home shortly after breakfast. It turns out that was not the case. He must have decided to enjoy Lake Castaic a bit longer."

"Thanks for your straightforward account, Mrs. Rhymes," said the sheriff. "Please send in your husband, if he's available."

CHAPTER 30

It was clear from the beginning that Ralph Rhymes took the questioning a personal insult. He tried to hide his resentment but did not succeed. When asked about his whereabouts on Wednesday morning, he stated, "At about nine o'clock I drove people to their chosen destinations on my golf cart."

"What people? Please be specific."

Ralph shrugged and said, "I gave the two ladies, Clarissa and Jaqueline, a ride to the swim beach. Vigo also hopped on board and got off at the fishing pier. Everyone else either walked or used their own form of transportation."

He continued, "Then I returned home and exchanged a light bulb that had burned out in the jumble room. After that, I spent some time with my computer. Later - - -"

The sheriff interrupted, asking, "What's a jumble room?"

"We call it that. It's where we keep extra stuff, like rollaway beds, sun umbrellas, folding chairs, and so forth."

"I see. Please continue."

"So later, I went out again to see if anyone needed me to get them to a different venue."

"At what time was that?"

"Approximately 11:00. I circled around the lake, knowing that sooner or later my services would be needed." He sighed and went on, "It was when I got close to the swim beach that I noticed smoke rising from behind a hill and at the same time heard sirens and, moments later, saw a chopper. Naturally, I needed to gather the guests and get them to The Vista, where I was sure they would be safe."

He paused, and since it was clear that the sheriff expected more, he said, "At the beach, the two women joined me and a bit farther down the lake, I stopped at the fishing pier to give Vigo a ride. Before crossing over to the upper lake, we found Hien, and I asked him to come on board too. That's about all I can tell you."

The sheriff asked, "What about the other guests?"

Clearly annoyed, Ralph replied, "In my mind, everyone was accounted for. With a blow of my whistle, I alerted Marvel, who was float-tube fishing, making him aware of the danger. We saw Enzo walking briskly toward the upper shore, obviously already aware of the fire. As we got close to home, May came driving from the opposite direction, looking for her husband. When she saw that he was with us, she turned around. The honeymooners spent the day at Magic Mountain, and at the time I thought that Tim had left the area."

As Ralph was let go, Sheriff Shaft glanced over to where Amanda sat. He smiled to himself when he noticed that she was already on the third page of her legal pad. The young woman seemed serious about note taking. Then he returned to the thought he had held in the back of his mind all through Ralph Rhymes' interview. He was sure that he knew the man but could not place him. Neither his name nor his face rang a bell, but he was convinced that the person was no stranger to him. Before the next suspect entered the room, he sent a text to his subordinate to do a background check on the owner of The Vista.

CHAPTER 31

Martina Padilla had an alarmed look on her face as she approached.

Trying to put her at ease, the sheriff said, "This is just routine questioning. I need to familiarize myself with the whereabouts of everyone on Wednesday morning, July 16." He looked down at his notes and continued, "Ms. Padilla, I don't have a home address for you; please provide it."

Martina thought, I can't afford him digging into my past and alerting my ex. She had to come up with something quickly and stuttered, "I was homeless."

The sheriff had a gut feeling that she was lying but let it slide. He smiled at her and said, "Good for you to have found such a nice place to stay."

When prompted to give an account of her movements on Wednesday morning, she said, "After putting the kitchen back in order following the guest's breakfast, I made up their rooms. The Asian gentleman stayed - - -"

"Would that be Hien Bong?"

"Yes."

"Sorry for interrupting," said the sheriff. "Please continue."

"Mr. Bong stayed in his room for breakfast, so I carried a tray to him. He didn't leave his room for a long time, so I couldn't get to making it up until close to eleven o'clock. When Mrs. Rhymes came back from shopping, I helped her put the groceries away."

Martina stopped her narrative and unclenched her fists, which she had kept tightened since the beginning of the questioning. She thought that the interview had come to an end but, looking the law enforcer in the eye, realized that her ordeal wasn't over yet.

She added, "I had plans to watch a movie but with all the excitement about the fire, I never got around to it."

"Ah, yes, let's get to the fire. How did you find out about it?"

"I was still in the kitchen with Mrs. Rhymes. We were expecting Mr. Rhymes for lunch and talked about what to fix when a helicopter flew above us, and a bit later we saw smoke. Soon Mr. Rhymes showed up but he wasn't alone. Some of the guests came with him and later the rest also arrived. Most hadn't touched their picnic lunch yet and ended up eating it in the dining room."

Sheriff Shaft said, "Thank you. That's all for the moment."

As Martina got up to leave, he added, "I take it you're not planning to change jobs any time soon?"

She shook her head and stated, "No. I love it here."

When the door closed behind the housekeeper, the sheriff looked over to where Amanda sat and remarked, "That woman is harboring a secret and I bet it has nothing to do with either the fire or Weinbau's murder. What do you think?"

"She looked scared as a rabbit is the only impression I got," came the answer.

Asher and Norice Jenkins entered the recreation room together. As a rule, the sheriff questioned suspects one at a time but decided to make an exception since he had been told that they were on their honeymoon. It soon became evident that they had nothing of importance to contribute. The pair had spent Wednesday at Magic Mountain, stating that they had left The Vista after breakfast at 8:45 a.m. and had returned around 6:00 p.m. Originally, their plans had been to stay at the amusement park longer and have dinner there, but when they became aware of the fire, they had decided to head back to Lake Castaic and their bed and breakfast earlier.

To the sheriff's question whether there were any witnesses to their statement, they said no but produced selfies taken at Magic Mountain.

He had no further questions but asked them not to leave the country any time soon.

CHAPTER 32

Jaqueline Blanchet was next and before Sheriff Shaft could utter a word, she beat him to it by saying, "When I came here to relax and take my mind off some personal problem, I didn't sign up to get interrogated in any arson and murder investigation."

Sheriff Shaft prompted, "Sorry for the inconvenience, but I'm sure you realize that I need to familiarize myself with each lodger's whereabouts on Wednesday morning."

"Not really," she prompted. "The fire could have been set by someone not staying at The Vista. The way I see it, the arsonist was caught red handed by Tim, who happened to be in the wrong place at the wrong time and was killed because of what he saw."

"I share your opinion that Mr. Weinbau's homicide was the result of what he witnessed, but questioning the guests here makes the most sense. You folks are not only suspects but could help me with the investigation by what you may have observed. So I'm starting with everyone here but not ruling out the possibility of an outsider being the perpetrator."

He continued, "Now then, let's have it. Where were you Wednesday morning?"

She shrugged her shoulders and replied, "Soon after breakfast, Mr. Rhymes gave us a ride to the swim beach in his golf cart. We stayed there until midday, when Mr. Rhymes drove up again and alerted us about a fire that broke out, and he gave us a ride back to the bed and breakfast."

"By 'us' you mean?"

"Clarissa and me."

The sheriff glanced at his list of names, then said, "Did you or Ms. Clever leave the swim beach at any time during the morning?"

"No, we swam and laid out there the entire time. - Wait! I used the restroom once."

"At what time was that?"

"I have no idea."

"During your morning at the beach, did you notice Tim Weinbau riding by on his bicycle, by any chance?"

"No, I didn't see him."

"That is all, Ms. Blanchet. Thanks for your cooperation, and please don't leave the country in the days to come," said the sheriff.

She rolled her eyes and got up to leave.

As the door closed behind her, Amanda asked, "Was she what they call in court 'a hostile witness'?"

The sheriff chuckled and said, "Not exactly, but she sure was not pleased about being questioned."

Then he drank a sip of water from the bottle Kate had provided before the next person stepped in.

CHAPTER 33

Clarissa Clever's statement was basically identical to her friend's account of Wednesday morning, with one exception. She was more precise about Jaqueline's restroom break.

When asked if she and Jaqueline stayed at the swim beach the entire morning, she answered in the affirmative at first. Then the sheriff said, "I understand that Ms. Blanchet left to use the restroom at one point."

"Oh, yes, I forgot about that."

"She was back in a flash, though?"

Clarissa hesitated for a couple of seconds with her response, realizing that it may not look good for her friend. She was tempted to say 'yes' but decided to stick to the truth, and she replied, "It took her a bit longer than expected."

"Oh?"

She was forced to elaborate, "The closest bathroom right on the swim beach was temporarily closed due to maintenance cleaning. Jaqueline couldn't wait and walked clear over to the one next to the fishing pier."

"Approximately how long did that take?"

Clarissa stated, "I wasn't timing it and didn't even wear a watch."

"Fair enough. But where was it in relation to the morning: beginning, mid-morning, or closer to noon?"

She hesitated for another second before answering, "It was closer to noon."

"During your time at the swim beach on Wednesday, did you encounter Tim Weinbau or any other guests of The Vista?"

"No, but that doesn't mean they couldn't have passed by without us noticing. Jaqueline and I were either swimming or laying out with our eyes closed."

"That makes sense," the sheriff agreed. Then he glanced down at his record and noticed the profession listed next to her name and said, "As a therapist, you must be a good judge of people."

He leaned in toward her and, lowering his voice, continued, "This is strictly between us, but do you have any suspicion as to our perpetrator?"

After the initial shock of his probing, she answered, "No, I have none. I do not analyze people unless they engage me professionally. Even then, I do not judge anyone."

The sheriff thought, she sure put me in my place. I must have violated some ethical code of hers. He was about to make an apologetic remark, but she didn't give him a chance. Glancing over to where Amanda sat, she stated, "But some of the guests would owe Tim an apology. His movements seemed suspicious at first and people in our group jumped to the wrong conclusion."

And then she addressed Amanda directly and said, "I'm sure I speak for everyone by saying, we are sorry."

The sheriff had no more questions and dismissed her.

Then he consulted the map that Mrs. Rhymes had provided and tried to judge the distance between the swim beach and the restrooms near the fishing pier.

CHAPTER 34

Marvel Maxwell appeared next and tried to hide his amusement as he looked over to where Amanda sat. Asher had informed him of her presence, but he could not help being entertained by witnessing the fact firsthand. Having the girlfriend of a murder victim 'sit in' on an investigation must be a first. Kudos to the sheriff for his unorthodox way of conducting his interrogations of murder suspects, Marvel thought.

As the sheriff's questioning took place, it became clear that Marvel's account of his movements on Wednesday tallied with what he had already learned from Ralph's earlier account.

But he wanted to hear it from this suspect himself and said, "So you had been float-tube fishing all Wednesday morning, correct?"

"Yes, sir."

"How did you get to the rental place?"

Marvel replied, "I walked." And clutching his small but protruding belly, he added, "As you can tell, I need the exercise."

"I'm unfamiliar with that type of fishing. How is it done?"

"It's simple. The inflatable little vessel is quite comfortable, and with your legs dangling off of the edge of the seat, you can waddle and move along the water. Needless to say that you can reach fishing places inaccessible from the shore. I had never done float-tube fishing before but found it relaxing and a great way to enjoy nature. As far as fish, I caught two small bass and tossed them back. I wasn't in the activity for food."

Sheriff Shaft asked, "At what time did you quit fishing?"

"I had planned to stay on the lake most of the day but was alerted about the fire and returned the float tube to the rental place as fast as I could. I'm not sure about the time but it must have been around noon or a bit later. Then I hightailed it back to The Vista, hoping the fire would burn in the opposite direction, which I learned later was the case."

"So you were alerted by the sirens of the fire engines and heard the helicopters?"

"No, sir. If you work in the city of L.A. like I do, you hear sirens on a regular basis. I've learned to tune them out. I did hear a helicopter and thought it was a nuisance, scaring the fish away. What really alerted me to the fire danger was Mr. Rhymes' loud whistle. It shocked me to the core and I looked in the direction from where the harsh sound came from. That is when I became aware of Mr. Rhymes sitting in his golf cart on the road parallel with the lake. He and his passengers pointed behind them, where I saw smoke rising from the back side of a small hill."

Marvel smiled and added, "I wasn't the only one who paid attention. Other folks out on the lake had obviously heard the whistle too and became aware of the fire. I saw them hurrying ashore also."

The sheriff could not think of anything else to ask him and ended the interview after advising him not to leave the country in the near future.

He looked over at Amanda's corner of the room while waiting for the next guest to enter and stated, "Now you know that a homicide investigation is tedious work, having to listen to lots of repetitions of facts."

"Unless some of it is not real fact," she remarked.

"Young woman, you are extremely wise for your age!"

CHAPTER 35

As Vigo Castelli entered, there was unmistakably what Sheriff Shaft would call a "continental swagger" in his stride. After what had already been established by Ralph Rhymes, Vigo confirmed that on Wednesday, he had gotten a ride to the fishing pier from the owner of The Vista and had stepped on board Ralph's golf cart again to return to the bed and breakfast after the fire had broken out.

"Sorry that your angler excursion came to such an abrupt end."

"Actually, I was bored with fishing. I don't seem to have the knack for it; they weren't biting. I only decided to fish because Enzo, my brother, wanted to do his own thing that day."

The sheriff didn't detect an accent and asked, "Judging by your first and last names, you and your brother must be at least second-generation Italian?"

"More like third. My grandparents had some influence in naming us," he replied with a grin.

Getting back in questioning mode, the sheriff continued, "I take it that you don't own any fishing gear. Did you rent the casting rod and bait?"

"I didn't have to. The Rhymes provide everything in their shed."

"Is that the small freestanding woodshed next to their house?"

"Correct," replied Vigo.

"Who handed you the equipment?"

"It's informal; you just help yourself. The only requirement they have is that you return things the way you found them."

"How convenient!"

That concluded the interview, and to the sheriff's standard warning about not leaving the country, Vigo answered, "As a matter of fact, I have plans to travel to Europe, Saturday the 26th, a week from today. I'm taking my family to England, France, and Switzerland before having to get ready for the new school year."

Sheriff Shaft handed him a card with his direct line and ordered, "Call me no later than July 22 with information and addresses of hotels or other places where you are planning to stay in each country."

"I'll do that," replied Vigo, and swaggered out of the room.

During that last interview, the sheriff had received a text from his subordinate. He looked at it now and mumbled, "Roland Pfadfinder! I'll be darned."

Amanda, who had excellent hearing, asked, "Who is Roland Pfadfinder?"

"He used to be a news anchor but I doubt you'd know him, being of a generation who doesn't get their news from TV."

CHAPTER 36

Noticing Enzo Castelli's stride as he approached the card table, the sheriff thought, here is that continental swagger again. But whereas his brother's gait was relaxed and looked natural, Enzo's version appeared full of tension.

Before sitting down, he glanced over at Amanda's corner and asked, "Is she a police officer?"

"No. Amanda is taking notes for me and won't disturb us. Now, tell me about 'your own thing' that you did on Wednesday, July 16," the sheriff started his questioning.

Enzo stared at him.

"Your brother mentioned that you did your own thing. What was that?"

"Oh, I see. Vigo suggested that we go kayaking on Wednesday, and I said I'd rather do some hiking and if I were lucky, I'd find some caterpillars to study. Since he wasn't interested in either activity, we went our separate ways on that day. We planned to do stuff together again on Thursday, but of course that didn't happen under the circumstances."

"I understand that there are plenty of hiking trails at the Lake Castaic area, but I'm curious what you mean by studying caterpillars."

"It's my hobby, which I find extremely interesting. I had spotted an area with California sagebrush at the lower lake earlier. Caterpillars love those bushes and if I were lucky, I'd find some cocoons, I thought."

"Thanks for clarifying," said the sheriff. "Now tell me your movements, step by step, on Wednesday, please."

"After breakfast I got a pair of trekking poles and a backpack out of the shed. I had ordered a picnic lunch, so I packed that, a bottle of water, and my magnifier in case I found caterpillars. And off I went. Temperatures were predicted to be in the mid-eighties by afternoon, so the morning promised not to be too hot."

He paused and thought back to his route on Wednesday, then continued, "I trekked on trails on the upper lake until reaching the dam, then crossed over to the lower lake. I ate part of my lunch early, resting at one of the picnic areas, and then I continued my hike. I passed the swim beach, and a few minutes later, I had arrived at those sagebrush bushes I remembered seeing the day before."

He beamed and went on, "I found three caterpillars and studied them. None had formed a cocoon yet, but I didn't give up hope. I was in the process of looking for more when I heard sirens. By the time I heard and then saw a helicopter, I looked up and noticed smoke rising from behind the small hill above me. I skipped my plan to eat the rest of my lunch someplace nearby and hurried back to The Vista."

The sheriff asked, "Did you encounter any of the guests during your hike?"

"I may have seen Clarissa and Jaqueline laying out at the beach, but it was from a distance, so I can't be sure it was them. I doubt that they saw me."

"Did you come across anyone else?"

"Later, on my way back to the bed and breakfast, Mr. Rhymes passed me in his golf cart. He had a bunch of passengers, including Vigo."

"Thanks for your detailed account," the sheriff said, and added his routine warning about not leaving the country.

Enzo said, "I have no plans of going abroad but am definitely moving to Texas next week."

The sheriff asked him to write down the Texas address before dismissing him.

CHAPTER 37

Mai Bong stuck her head in the door and hesitated.

"Come on in and have a seat," said the sheriff, while pointing to the chair vacated by Enzo seconds earlier.

Glancing in Amanda's direction and meeting with an encouraging smile, she sat down.

Prompted about her movements on Wednesday morning she said, "My husband didn't feel up to leaving our room for breakfast, so I went to the dining room by myself. While there, I asked Clarissa, the therapist, if I could hire her to help Hien, but she said that would be unprofessional here, while we were all vacationing. Also, she was fully booked for months ahead but gave me info about a colleague she highly recommended.

"Anyhow, after getting back to our room, I tried to get Hien interested in exploring activities around the lake, but he didn't feel up to it. I couldn't even persuade him to a game of pickleball, so I ventured out by myself."

The sheriff asked, "There's a pickleball court in the park?"

"No, but there is one in a town close by; we googled it. Hien loves the sport."

"Is your husband ill?"

"Not exactly. I believe 'depressed' is the word people use."

It was evident to the sheriff that the tension coming from this suspect revolved around her spouse. He decided to leave that subject alone and got to the point by asking, "So you left The Vista alone. On foot?"

"No, I took the car, as I planned to venture into the entire area."

He looked her in the eye and waited.

After what seemed like a long pause, she said, "You want me to tell you exactly where I went?"

"Please!"

"I first explored the upper lake. I parked near the rental place, sat on a bench for a while and watched the jet skiers go by. A bit farther up, I observed a water skier. He was pretty good, doing all sorts of tricks. Then I drove parallel with a hiking trail for a bit and suddenly people on horseback crossed the road right in front of me. Luckily, I was safely in the car; I'm deathly afraid of horses."

She continued, "Later, I drove to the end of the lake and crossed over to the lower lagoon, where - - -"

"You crossed near the dam?" asked the sheriff who had followed her movements on his map.

"No, we did that the previous day. On Wednesday, I made a U-turn after the scare with the horses, since I was afraid that I might encounter more horseback riders if I kept going. I drove in the opposite direction and crossed at the other end of the lake."

"Sorry, please go on."

"Where was I?" she said. And after a brief pause, she resumed, "People were fishing at the lower lagoon, but that's kind of boring, so I didn't stop to watch. When I came across a children's playground, I parked and observed a toddler and his mom at the slide and swings for a while."

Mai paused again and reflected for a few seconds before continuing, "As I explored a remote area, I suddenly felt guilty about having left my husband to fend for himself and decided to drive back to the bed and breakfast, so that we could have lunch together. I made a wrong turn and got a bit lost, ending up at the road's end. When I turned the car around and headed back where I'd come from, I saw Tim on his bicycle."

She stopped and said, "But I already told this to Amanda. We even went there and I showed her the exact area."

Sheriff Shaft agreed, "I know, but please tell us again."

"Like I mentioned to Amanda, Tim had his back to me, riding up a small hill. I'm sure he didn't see me."

"At what time was that?"

"Shortly before noon. I didn't look at my watch but had looked at it moments before when it was 11:45."

"With only seeing his back, are you sure it was Tim Weinbau?"

"Positive. I recognized his helmet and his backpack. They were both turquoise. Tim had his own backpack. The ones available in the shed are all brown."

"You are very observant." And he asked, "Did you notice anyone else in that area?"

"No. Only Tim," she replied.

"Please continue."

"Like I said, I was heading back to The Vista, but when I arrived, my husband wasn't in our room, nor anywhere else on the property. At that point I heard a helicopter and seconds later saw smoke rising from somewhere at the lower lake area."

She took a deep breath and went on, "That's when I panicked with worry and drove off again, looking for him. I thanked God when I saw him safe with Mr. Rhymes in the golf cart, going in the opposite direction. Of course I turned around and also headed back to the bed and breakfast."

The sheriff asked, "When you went to The Vista looking for Mr. Bong, did you see anyone else there?"

"Yes. Since Hien wasn't in our room, I searched the entire house. When I opened the kitchen door, I found Mrs. Rhymes and the housekeeper there. They didn't know where Hien went but the housekeeper said that he left the room around 11 o'clock."

"Thank you for your precise statement, Mrs. Bong. Please send your husband in now," said the sheriff.

He waited until the door closed behind Mai, then looked over to Amanda's corner and asked, "Tim liked the color turquoise?"

"It matched his eyes," she replied, trying not to choke up.

CHAPTER 38

Hien Bong was polite and cooperative but there was a vacant stare to his eyes that was disconcerting. His answers came automatically and without hesitation but lacked emotion.

Initially, his account of Wednesday morning tallied with that of his wife, that he ate his breakfast in his room and didn't join her on her outing.

"Why not?" asked the sheriff.

"I didn't feel like it."

After a long silence it became clear that the man was not going to elaborate further, so the sheriff prompted, "But you left your room later, right?"

He nodded.

"At what time was that?"

"I don't know."

"But you left not only your room but also The Vista?"

"Yes."

This is like pulling teeth, the sheriff thought, and asked, "Why did you venture out?"

"The housekeeper knocked at the door, wanting to make up the room."

"At what time?"

"I don't know."

The sheriff demanded, "Tell me where you went after leaving your room and please be precise."

"I went to the shed and fetched a pair of trekking poles, since my wife said they might help with my leg."

"What's wrong with your leg?"

"Not much. I have an old injury which acts up when I walk," came the reply.

"So you went for a hike?" prompted the sheriff, thinking that he had finally made progress with the questioning of this suspect.

"More like a walk."

"Where did you go?"

"No place in particular. I walked along the main road leading around the lake. After a while, my leg was bothering me, so I sat down near the lake until Mr. Rhymes gave me a ride back to the bed and breakfast."

"I take it that you were aware of a fire that broke out in the area?"

"Not until Mr. Rhymes told me so and insisted that I hop on board his golf cart."

Looking at the information the sheriff had for each suspect, he said, "You're an IT specialist, correct?"

"Yes."

"Do you like your job?"

"I hate it!"

The answer had come with such sudden force that the law enforcer thought it best not to pursue the subject and concluded the interview, but not before mentioning his routine warning about not leaving the country.

That finished the list of people he needed to interview. Amanda counted 19 handwritten pages of her record taking.

She stated, "I'll type it all up and send it to you in an email attachment."

"You don't have to do that."

"I know, but I want to."

The sheriff understood that she needed to get involved as part of her healing process and said, "In that case, thank you!" And he added, "Ready to go on a field trip this afternoon?"

"To the scene of the crime?" she wanted to know.

"Exactly."

CHAPTER 39

Kate entered the recreation room and asked Sheriff Shaft if all guests were free to go home. The way she put it was, "Most were booked including tomorrow, but under the circumstances and with the bad air and all, they are anxious to leave."

"By all means," he replied, "they can go home. I may have further questions but know where and how to reach everybody. That reminds me, is Mr. Rhymes handy? I'd like another word with him, please."

"I'll look for him," she replied.

"And, Mrs. Rhymes, I would like to order a picnic lunch for Ms. Redding and myself, if that's not too much trouble."

"Not at all. Turkey and Swiss cheese is today's sandwich. Is that okay?"

"Sounds delicious."

We'll have it ready in a few minutes," she said, and rushed off.

The expression on Ralph's face as he entered could be interpreted as 'what now?'

The sheriff said, "I'd like to familiarize myself as to where everyone was at the crucial time. Mr. Bong was vague in his statement." And indicating the map in front of him, he requested, "Show me where you found him and asked him to come on board."

Ralph pointed to a water's edge area close to the lower lake fishing pier, stating, "Right around here."

Then he pinned the sheriff with a mocking stare and inquired, "Is the exact location really important?"

"It could be," came the reply.

The sheriff thanked him for his time and dismissed him.

CHAPTER 40

They drove in the law enforcer's unmarked car to the lower lake area. After they arrived at the isolated spot where the roads forked, the sheriff parked on the dead-end street where Mai had turned around on the day of the fire.

They walked along the path that Tim had taken on his bicycle up that fateful hill, stopped and stared up the small slope, then trekked the short distance to the top.

As they surveyed the devastation down the back side of the slope, Amanda stated, "Nothing has changed since I stood here on Thursday, looking at the fire's destruction. The "Restricted area:Keep out" sign is still here. The only difference is that the fire investigation team I saw that day is no longer around."

The sheriff said, "I'm sure their work is still ongoing. They may be taking their lunch break right now. And don't forget, this is Saturday; there's a good chance that they have the weekend off."

Still staring down at the burned range, Amanda remarked, "Lucky that the brush fire burned away from any structures and recreational areas of the park and not in the opposite direction."

The sheriff prompted, "Maybe luck had nothing to do with it. There wasn't any strong wind to make the flames jump, and the arsonist seems to have known his business by making the fire burn away from the popular and most frequented section of the park."

Then he stated, "There is nothing for us to do up here. Let's walk back down and you can show me where you found Tim's phone."

Amanda did just that. She stopped near one of the bushes a few yards above the road that led around the lake. Pointing to it, she stated, "The phone was hidden under this one. I would have never seen it if it hadn't been for the ringing."

"Ah yes, I meant to ask you. What made you dial Tim's number? Did you expect to find his phone?"

"I sort of dialed it by accident," and a bit embarrassed, she told him about her sudden wish to see her boyfriend in an old video.

"That was a lucky accident," he said with a grin.

He instantly got serious again and assessed their immediate surroundings and remarked, "There sure are a lot of shrubs and bushes in this entire area. Is any of it sagebrush?"

"I don't know. I'm not into plants," she admitted.

He stooped to examine one of the species, then said, "I'll be darned. There are caterpillars on this bush."

They walked on, crossed the road, then stopped by the sandy shore. The bicycle tracks leading down to the lake were still visible, but barely so. Both stood there, each lost in their own musing. Amanda thought, oh Tim! Why didn't you ride out of here right after sending that text? The sheriff, for his part, dwelled on the fact that riding a bicycle into a lake made no sense, no matter what the circumstances.

He finally asked, "Tim knew how to swim, right?"

"Definitely. He was a good swimmer."

The sheriff stared into the water and then stated, "In this area, there is a huge drop near the lake's edge where there is great depth right away as opposed to other parts where it gradually deepens. I learned that fact from the workers who retrieved the bicycle from the bottom of the lake."

He continued, "I briefly talked with the coroner at the time the body was discovered and hope to get his full report soon. I'm counting on the fact that the medical examiner's findings will shed some light on this case. It would help to know in what condition the victim's body was before he drowned. I imagine that a severe wound to the head may have made him disoriented."

As soon as the sentence left his mouth, he realized whom he was talking to and regretted his choice of words. He glanced at her and noticed a slight flinch of the eye, but she quickly had herself in control again.

He looked at his watch and then suggested, "I hope you don't mind doing your own sleuthing for a bit. What I'd like you to do is walk at a steady pace to the swim beach and time yourself. Meanwhile, I'll time my walks to the fishing pier, the float-tube rental place, and the spot where Mr. Bong hung out. Then I'll drive the car to the picnic area nearest the swim beach where we'll meet up, compare notes, and have lunch."

"Sounds like a plan," she said, and they went their separate ways.

CHAPTER 41

Amanda reached the designated place first and sat down at a table under the shade of a coast live oak tree. The picnic area was not crowded, which wasn't surprising. Most people stayed away from the State Park at this point to avoid the unhealthy air still lingering from the fire. There was only one other table and benches occupied by a family with small children at the opposite end. She was sure they were far enough away to allow privacy for the powwow between her and the sheriff.

When Sheriff Shaft arrived, he said, "I'm starved. Let's eat first," as he unpacked their lunches.

The temperature had climbed to near 90 degrees and Amanda was not hungry, but she eagerly drank the bottled water Mrs. Rhymes had added to the cooler bag and forced herself to take a few bites from the sandwich.

Nourished and ready to proceed, the sheriff asked, "So how much time did your walk take to the swim beach?"

"Nine minutes," she said. "I'm sure you wanted me to time it because of Jaqueline's alleged walk to the restroom."

"Correct. So it would have taken her 18 minutes to walk to and back from the spot where you and I separated. And, let's say, a total of three more minutes to hike up and back down the little slope, plus another minute to get the fire started. That would be a total of 22 minutes. The bathroom near the fishing pier is only a three-minute walk from the lakeshore where you and I parted. So it would have taken her roughly about the same time to use the restroom."

Amanda said, "Theoretically, she could have started the fire instead of looking for a bathroom."

He smiled and agreed, "Theoretically, yes. And of course, theoretically, if she went to the bathroom as she stated, her friend, Clarissa Clever, was left alone at the beach and could have taken that time to walk over and up that hill and start the fire."

He paused, then stated, "As to my own walking experience, like I just mentioned, the fishing pier is only a three-minute walk away from where Tim's bicycle tracks led into the lake. The float-tube rental place is an eight-minute walk away, and the spot where Mr. Bong was found by Mr. Rhymes is 11 minutes away on foot. I checked with the man at the rental place. Marvel returned his float tube at 12:20. As you saw for yourself, the sagebrush bushes grow all over the area around the path leading up the little hill. So I assume Mr. Castelli was looking for caterpillars in that region, which would also be three minutes away."

"Do you know the time when the fire started?"

"It was reported by a horseback rider in a call to 911 at 12:05 p.m. The exact time when it started is unknown. As you gathered during their interviews, people were vague as to the time they did things, let alone when they became aware of the fire."

Amanda reached into her large bag and, rifling through her legal sheet records, said, "Let's see who we can eliminate. Asher and Norice, for sure. They spent the entire day at Magic Mountain."

Sheriff Shaft shook his head and said, "It's far-fetched, but they could have left the amusement park early. The selfie they showed me was taken there sometime in the morning."

Following some more paper shuffling she said, "Marvel was on the lake float-tube fishing and returned his equipment at 12:20, like you just said. So he was definitely still on the lake when the fire was set."

"True, and Mr. Rhymes saw him on the lake while chauffeuring guests back to the bed and breakfast. But here again, he could have stopped earlier, left the tube somewhere at the water's edge, commit the crime, and return back to his fishing within a few minutes."

"What about Mrs. Rhymes? Surely we can eliminate her. She came back from her grocery shopping trip at - -" she searched for the correct page in her notes - - "after 11:30, probably closer to 12:00. Also, we have the housekeeper confirm it."

The sheriff said, "Correct. But she could have swung by the lower lake area first, done the crime, then drove home with her groceries. That goes for Martina Padilla too, by the way. We don't know what she did before joining Mrs. Rhymes in the kitchen."

"I'm positive we can at least cross Mai off the suspect list," said Amanda. "She's the one that came forward and told me that she saw Tim at the crucial time. She even drove me to the spot where she noticed him bicycling up that hill. If not for her, I wouldn't have searched for clues in the right area and neither his bike nor Tim would have been found."

"Oh, but if she is our perpetrator, going out of her way to help you would have been a clever move. She had to assume that, sooner or later, there would be a search for Tim, and his body and bicycle would be found. Being accommodating to you by showing the spot where she saw Tim would make her look innocent. Don't forget, she couldn't have known that you would find Tim's phone. She may not even have realized that he either lost it or tossed it into the bush on purpose."

"So we can't exclude anyone?"

"I'm afraid not."

The family at the other end of the picnic area got ready to leave. Amanda watched as the parents gathered their trash and disposed of it in the nearest bin, then rounded up their kids. The children's happy chatter could be heard as they made their way past them. Amanda couldn't help thinking that she wished to be this carefree.

The sheriff said, "My biggest problem with this case is reconstructing how or why your boyfriend rode his bicycle into the lake. You can't kill someone and then sit him back on the bike. On the other hand, carrying a body and pushing it into the lake, then riding the bike and jumping off before it hits the water, would have taken a lot of effort and time. Besides, the perpetrator could not afford to be seen doing all that, so that scenario is out of the question. Yet, we have to deal with the bicycle tracks leading right into the water. As I said before, maybe the coroner's findings will shed light on it."

Neither one spoke for a while. Then Amanda broke the silence and said, "I guess it's possible that the culprit is a stranger, unknown to the bed and breakfast crowd."

"Sure, it's possible but highly improbable. A complete stranger would have had other options."

"What do you mean?"

"Had the arsonist been unknown to Tim, he could have averted his face, then fled, possibly down the other side of the hill where the fire was headed. I doubt that Tim would have risked pursuing someone under those circumstances. And chances are slim that he could have identified the person in a line-up."

"You've given this some thought," was Amanda's comment.

He continued, "The first things we look into in a criminal case are motive and alibi. The motive in this murder is self-preservation. The killer could not risk being identified as an arsonist, let alone the Southland Torcher. As to alibis, none of the suspects have a foolproof one."

"So where do we go from here?"

"We sleep on it. I'll drive you back to The Vista and then you go home and do whatever relaxes you," replied the sheriff.

And after a pause he added, "As far as helping me with the investigation, I thank you, but from now on I'll work on the case alone. Don't worry, I'll keep in touch and inform you of the final outcome."

With dread, Amanda spent the entire time on her drive home to Sherman Oaks anticipating the phone call she would have to make to Tim's folks in Florida. How does one tell parents that their son has been murdered, she wondered.

CHAPTER 42

Most guests were anxious to leave. As the Jenkinses had left Castaic behind and drove south on Interstate 5, Norice said, "I misjudged Tim and am sorry about that. I tagged him as the villain and he turned out to be the victim."

"Try not to dwell on it," remarked Asher. And he added, "I'm sorry we had such a bad experience on our honeymoon. Let's head down to the beach and spend the rest of our vacation there. If we can't find a hotel or motel with a vacancy, we'll drive home tonight and go back tomorrow."

Norice leaned toward the driver seat and, laying her head on his shoulder, proclaimed, "You always have such good ideas. I'm glad I married you!"

The Castelli brothers were checking out of The Vista too. They scarcely talked and listened to classic rock while driving home in Vigo's Honda. Each man was lost in his own musing.

A few miles before dropping his brother off in Burbank, Vigo said, "Sorry that our stay at Castaic Lake was cut short, but we spent some quality time together in spite of it all."

"True, and this extra day gives me more time to pack and do last minute stuff here," Enzo replied.

"Call me if you need help with anything. Rachel and the kids won't come home until Monday, so I'm basically free for the rest of the weekend."

"Thanks!"

After they arrived at Enzo's apartment, the brothers gave one another a quick hug, barely touching. Enzo grabbed his bag out of the trunk of the car, and as he walked toward the building's entrance, his brother called out after him in true Texan style, "Don't be a stranger and give me a jingle sometime, ya hear!"

The Bongs were also on their way home. They drove in silence all the way to their home in La Cañada Flintridge. Mai had tried to engage her husband in conversation, but it was no use. She tuned in to a classical music station but neither her ears nor her mind found any pleasure in it. She had hoped that a week of relaxation at the bed and breakfast would help Hien's depression, but now it seemed worse than ever. She felt as though the man she'd been married to for decades had become a total stranger to her.

By the time they reached their home, Mai had made up her mind to call the therapist that Clarissa Clever had recommended, first thing Monday morning.

Jaqueline and Clarissa had driven to The Vista in separate cars, so Clarissa hugged her friend good-bye on Saturday afternoon with the promise, "See you someday soon. And don't forget what we talked about: Turn your back to the past and start anew."

Then she returned to the recreation room, where Marvel challenged her to a game of chess.

In the Rhymes' living room a heated conversation took place.

Kate said, "So far none of the new guests for the coming week have cancelled. I sure hope it stays that way."

"Why do you expect cancellations?" asked Ralph.

"Think about it! There was mention in the paper about Tim Weinbau's homicide investigation. From their point of view The Vista might have housed a murderer."

"Now you're getting dramatic. That's absurd."

"There is also the bad air quality to consider. I bet people will cancel for that reason too. We can't afford to have the place only half full or even empty. We put too much money into The Vista and need to have it running at full capacity."

"You are getting hysterical for no reason. Nobody has cancelled yet and I doubt that anyone will. All you care about is your precious bed and breakfast. I'm sick of the place already!" yelled Ralph, and slammed the door on his way out.

CHAPTER 43

It turned out that the chess players were well matched and able to concentrate on the game while holding a conversation between, or even during, a move.

Clarissa said, "I think we're the only guests left. People blamed the unhealthy air for cutting their stay short but, no doubt, they got scared of sticking around with a murderer in our midst."

"My point exactly," said Marvel, and he teased, "So how come you're not afraid of sticking around with me?"

She moved her knight and was obviously flirting when saying, "I'll take my chances."

He made a countermove with his bishop and said, "Seriously, have you given the suspect matter any thought?"

"I have my suspicions, but I'll keep them to myself for now. How about you?"

He smiled and said, "True to your profession, you most likely made your pick by analyzing each guest's psyche."

She nodded while moving her other knight.

"I, on the other hand, am looking at it from an alibi point of view. I'm positive we can eliminate the newlyweds. Suggesting that they took a break from Magic Mountain in the middle of the day is too far-fetched. Everyone else was at the Lake Castaic State Park at the time the fire was set and therefore has no alibi."

Clarissa asked, "What do you make of Tim's girlfriend joining Sheriff Shaft in his investigation?"

"I doubt that you can call it 'joining' him in his work. He just let her sit in as he interviewed us all. She was sitting quietly in her corner during my questioning, and I assume that was the case for everyone."

"Sure, but just letting her be there is unorthodox in a criminal investigation, I would think."

Marvel said, "It may be unorthodox, but I give him credit for allowing it. I also think that he knows a smart cookie when he sees one. And for the young woman's part, I admire the brave face she puts on, given her predicament."

They concentrated on their game and stayed silent for several moves, while they each captured some of their opponent's chess pieces.

Then Clarissa remarked, "I'm planning to drive home today but am in no hurry. I live in Studio City, only a half hour's drive away." And she added, "According to your business card, your chiropractor practice is in the City of L.A., but where do you live? Or is that too personal a question?"

"Not at all. Manhattan Beach is my town of residence."

"That's a beach town I don't know well. I think I've only been there once," she stated, while lining her queen up with his king and calling "Check."

He moved the king out of danger and replied, "I'll be happy to show you around someday."

Already at breakfast that first day Marvel had noticed that Clarissa's ring finger was bare. She was left-handed and now, while moving her chess pieces around the board, he was aware of it again.

He asked, "Have you ever been married?"

"No, but I was engaged once and he got cold feet and called it off one week before the wedding."

"He must have felt threatened by your sharp intellect!"

She grinned and said, "You've got that right." And she asked, "What about you and marriage?"

"So far, I haven't come across the right woman."

Clarissa made her last move with her rook, cornering his king with no place to go and announced, "*Checkmate!*"

"Wow," he said, "you checkmated me in less than 40 moves. I'm impressed."

He thought, I take back my opinion that all shrinks have mental issues of their own. This one clearly does not fall into that category.

They exchanged phone numbers before being the last of the guests to leave The Vista.

CHAPTER 44

On Sunday morning, July 20, Sheriff Shaft said to his wife, "How about that day at the beach I promised you? With the boys spending a week back East with my folks, it's just you and me."

"I thought you were busy with a murder case," she replied.

"It's Sunday, and I'm taking the day off. I'm stuck with the investigation until I get the coroner's report. And, since I do my best detecting applying my brain, I might as well do that at the beach."

Two hours later, they had spread out their blanket and erected their sun umbrella in the sand at Huntington Beach. They took turns swimming in the ocean so as not to leave their stuff unattended. The sheriff watched his wife, way out beyond the surf, swimming parallel with the shore. She had always been drawn to water like a fish. In their younger days, she had even surfed, something he had tried and failed at.

The beach was crowded on this hot weekend day, with many people in the water, but no one swam out as far as his wife. He finally lost track of where she was and closed his eyes. There were no rip currents as far as he could tell, and even if she should be caught in one, she knew what to do.

As soon as he relaxed, his mind went immediately into detective mode and the Tim Weinbau case. True to her word, Amanda had emailed him the records she had taken during the guests' questioning. He had looked them over briefly the night before but planned to study them methodically later. He was aware that he was missing an important fact but could not put his finger on it yet.

Taking into account that he was most likely dealing with the Southland Torcher, he knew where the suspects lived and their professions. They all resided in Southern California and, since all recent fires were set in that general region, everyone on his list of perpetrators had had easy access to the crime scenes. Figuring out where every person was when each fire broke out would involve a great deal of research. He hoped that it would not come to that tedious task. After all, solving the murder of Tim Weinbau was in essence his only job.

He opened his eyes and looked out to sea. He spotted his wife still further out than the surf but now swimming toward the shore. It was good to know that she was on her way back. The sheriff had never admitted to her nor to anyone else that he was always a bit uneasy when she swam far out into the ocean.

He shut his eyes again and returned to his musing. He pictured each individual during their interview in the recreation room, concentrating not on what they said but their demeanor. Many had things to hide, but it might have had nothing to do with the crime.

Changing gear in his mind's eye, he concentrated on the golf cart. He had already googled its speed and knew that it could run as fast as 25 miles per hour. It might be a good idea to inquire if Ralph Rhymes's cart ran on gas or electricity. He needed to pay The Vista an additional visit and most likely have another talk with some of the suspects.

The soothing smell of the ocean, the pleasant warmth of the sun on his body, and the steady chatter of kids building a sandcastle nearby almost lulled him to sleep.

He jumped at the wet touch of his wife's hand on his shoulder as she said, "Let's eat, I'm starved."

Toweling herself off, then grabbing her beach bag, she handed him a bottle of water and said, "I'm having half a sandwich. Do you want a whole or half?"

"I'm not on a diet. Make it a whole and your other half too," he replied with a grin.

CHAPTER 45

The coroner's report landed on Sheriff Shaft's desk first thing on Monday morning. He read it through with great care a couple of times. Paying no attention to the medical jargon it amounted to the following:

Healthy 23-year-old male. Death by drowning. Date and time of death, Wednesday, July 16 between 11:45 a.m. and 12:45 p.m. Significant head injury and trauma to the left temple, executed before the body entered the water. The wound could have been inflicted by a sharp object, a heavy rock, or even a person's fist. The blow would have had to come with great force to cause the severe injury. Otherwise the individual was in excellent shape before expiring.

Added at the bottom of the report the coroner wrote a personal note to Sheriff Shaft. It read, "*In my opinion, the severe head wound may have rendered the victim either semi-conscious, unconscious, or disoriented. He could also have been blinded by the large amount of blood flowing from his wound.*

There we have it, thought the sheriff. The mystery about how Tim Weinbau rode his bike into the lake was solved. If he were barely conscious and disoriented, it would make sense that he desperately held on to stay in the saddle. And if he was blinded, he had no idea that the bike was headed for the water until it was too late. Being disoriented would make even an excellent swimmer lose direction and swim downward instead of toward the surface. It is a fact that the lake is deep at the location where the bike was found.

He thought, knowing what that sharp object was would be a great clue. The thing was obviously the murder weapon. It could not have been a fist; he had scrutinized the suspects' hands during their interviews. None showed any sign of a fistfight.

Then he printed out Amanda's notes and spent most of the day studying each suspect's account of their whereabouts on Wednesday, July 16, paying particular attention to the crucial time just before the brush fire was reported by the horseback rider.

After going through each person's statement for the umpteenth time, nothing essential came to mind, and he gave up for the time being. To relax and take his mind off the case, he thought back to the beach outing of the previous day and their teasing banter before eating a picnic lunch. The question his wife had posed, "Do you want a whole or half sandwich?" suddenly triggered something in his memory.

He followed up on that thought, then checked Amanda's interview notes once more. And there he found that clue he had missed, a fact that had been nagging at him at the back of his mind. Now he realized what he had been overlooking all along.

He checked two people's statements again. Sure enough, there was a discrepancy which stood out like a sore thumb. He could not understand why he had failed to spot it before. One person was lying. It remained to be determined which one. Seconds later, he tapped his forehead with the realization that he knew exactly who the liar was!

Studying the interview records one last time, the sheriff knew who the perpetrator was. Proving it, however, was a tricky matter. He needed to tread carefully, as he could not afford a wrong move at this point in time.

Another visit to The Vista was indicated. There remained a good chance that evidence could still be found at the bed and breakfast. A close look at their woodshed was necessary, and the sheriff made the proper arrangements.

CHAPTER 46

It was Monday, shortly after lunch, when Kate opened the door to Ralph's study and announced, "Sheriff Shaft is back with a whole bunch of his minions. I sure hope he is done before our new guests arrive. They are searching the shed, and he - -"

Ralph looked up from the monitor, jumped to his feet, then raced past her and out the door, grunting, "What the devil does he want from our shed?"

The sound on the computer was turned down but out of the corner of her eye Kate noticed movement on the large computer monitor screen. Curious about the video, she stepped closer, and an involuntary screech escaped her, as she got the shock of her life. Moments later, shaking and pale as a ghost, she left the study.

She found the sheriff in the hallway talking with her husband, saying, "There is no reason to get alarmed, Mr. Rhymes. Searching the shed is basically a formality. We need to take all possibilities into account. The forensic team will be in and out of there in no time, I promise."

He noticed Kate coming onto the scene and said, "While the members of the team are doing their thing, maybe we three can have a chat in the recreation room, if convenient?"

Ralph reluctantly agreed and Kate nodded mechanically while her mind was racing.

Once seated in the recreation room, the sheriff turned to Ralph and said, "I'm aware that you are Roland Pfadfinder, but legally changing one's name is not against the law. I want you to know that I don't hold this against you, and that I will keep that knowledge to myself."

Not giving Ralph a chance to comment, the sheriff continued, "I had a quick peek into the shed before the team members took over. Tell me, Mr. Rhymes, does your golf cart run on gas or electricity?"

"Gas," was the reply.

"That explains the can of gasoline I noticed, which didn't seem to belong among the casting rods, bait, trekking poles, backpacks, and other recreational equipment."

Ralph could not keep the sarcasm out of his voice as he said, "I take it that is not against the law either."

"Correct," replied the sheriff with a grin, then turned to Kate.

He had planned to ask her whether she could remember the time her husband and his passengers had arrived at The Vista after the fire was discovered. But, glancing her way, he was alarmed and asked instead, "Are you okay?" The lady was white as snow and visibly upset.

She touched her forehead with a shaking hand, as if to erase what was on her mind, and answered, "Just a bit of a headache. Sorry!"

The sheriff decided not to pose Kate any questions at that point. They were not important. The poor woman looked like she was in either physical or mental agony. He basically needed to kill time until the forensics were through in the shed. Having more questions for the pair was only an excuse to linger. He engaged Ralph in a bit of small talk, but the conversation was lopsided, since the gentleman was not in a talkative mood. He was relieved when he received a text from the team letting him know that they were wrapping things up. Thanking the Rhymeses for their time, he got up and left.

Out in the shed, the forensic experts found what they were looking for and ran initial testing on the spot. Then they packed the item up, making sure not to contaminate it, and carried it to their vehicle for transportation to their lab, where it would be further analyzed and DNA tested. Eventually, the item would be submitted as evidence.

CHAPTER 47

There was a rush order out to the lab technicians. Still, at least a day or two would pass before Sheriff Shaft would be in possession of the results. In the meantime, he needed to find a way to get his main suspect's DNA. In order not to alert that person, and also to properly eliminate all other suspects, he asked everyone concerned to come to the sheriff's station for another talk.

When he called all the suspects late Monday afternoon, he phrased his summons this way: "I need to take down everyone's statement one more time to complete my investigation. It is urgent, so please come to the Castaic Sheriff Station tomorrow."

His phone orders to all concerned were not welcome and he understood that, except for Ralph and Kate Rhymes and Martina Padilla, their housekeeper, who resided nearby, driving back to Castaic was an inconvenience. Some were more reluctant to do so than others. A few stated that they could not take time out from their job, others claimed to have prior commitments, and Enzo said that he was too busy taking care of things before his move to Texas. The sheriff reminded them that this was official business which took priority. In the end, everyone complied, realizing that a 'no show' would make them look guilty.

They trickled in at the sheriff's station one by one or in pairs on Tuesday morning. He did not use the interrogation room. Instead, he held the interviews in his small office, adjacent to the officer's launch, where each person waited their turn.

He had set the thermostat to 80 degrees in his office on that hot summer day, making sure everyone was perspiring. He apologized for the heat, claiming that the air conditioning was temporarily out of order in that room. Then he offered them a paper cup of water from the cooler while getting their statements. As soon as each person left, he dropped their empty cup into an evidence bag, pre-marked with each of their names. He felt certain that there would be enough saliva from their lips and/or sweat from their hands for a DNA sample.

As to their statements, they were not important, since they basically confirmed what each person had said during their previous interviews. Some varied a bit, but that had to be expected after the time lapse. Vigo handed him a piece of paper and said that, rather than phoning him the info about his European itinerary, he had decided to bring it in writing.

The only testimony the sheriff paid close attention to was the one his prime suspect gave. Sure enough, the culprit made that same blunder again when describing their movements at Castaic Lake on Wednesday, July 16. This time, though, the gaffe got the sheriff's attention immediately.

By Wednesday afternoon, July 23, exactly one week after the fire and Tim Weinbau's drowning, Sheriff Shaft was in possession of all the lab findings, including the DNA results. Thanks to the speedy efforts of the forensics team and the lab technicians' willingness to work overtime, he could now proceed with the case.

At the same time, Tim Weinbau's body could be released to his parents, who had flown in from Florida.

CHAPTER 48

At his apartment in Burbank, Enzo was getting ready to leave for Texas first thing the next morning. He planned to drive and only take along what would fit into his SUV: in other words, no furniture and just his bare necessities. His suitcases and bags were packed, except for last-minute toiletries.

As of the next day, his electricity, gas, water, and trash pickup would be shut off.. Most of his furniture had been either sold or donated. What was left would be hauled away by the owner of the building.

Enzo was reflecting that he would start fresh in Texas, professionally, personally, and in every other respect, leaving bad habits behind. It was only fitting that he would purchase new furniture when starting a fresh chapter of his life. He was getting excited about what lay ahead. And if luck would have it, he may even find love.

His thoughts were interrupted when the doorbell rang. Must be the Salvation Army to pick up the desk I promised them, he thought, as he opened the door.

"Oh, it's you, Sheriff Shaft! Come on in. Sorry I can't offer you a chair to sit in. As you can see, my furniture is mostly gone," Enzo said.

"This won't take long," said the sheriff as he stepped into the living room.

"I hope you're getting close to solving your homicide investigation, but I doubt that I can help you further. I told you all I know."

"I'm not just close, I solved it. And as far as telling me all you know, you left a whole bunch of it out. On the other hand, you told me too much."

"I don't understand."

The sheriff stated, "Telling me about being equipped with a magnifier and pointing out those sagebrush bushes, for instance, was a huge mistake."

"I don't know what you mean."

"Sure you do. That caterpillar hobby of yours came in handy and fooled me at first, but in the end I saw through it all."

Enzo said, "You can't seriously think that I'm responsible for Tim's death."

"I don't think so; I know so. Your DNA is all over the murder weapon and so is the victim's blood."

"But I - - -"

Enzo realized the blunder and did not finish the sentence.

The sheriff finished it for him and stated, "Yes, you wiped it clean, you thought. But our forensic fellows have a way to detect blood invisible to the naked eye. And what's more, they can analyze it for blood type and DNA."

He pointed to the suitcases standing all around the room and said, "You won't need these where you're headed." Then he pulled out a pair of handcuffs from his back pocket and formally announced, "Enzo Castelli, I place you under arrest for the murder of Tim Weinbau."

Enzo was no fool. He had known the purpose of the sheriff's visit the minute the law enforcer had stepped into his apartment. The useless chatter he had put forward was to mentally prepare himself for what was coming.

CHAPTER 49

After Sheriff Shaft and the forensic team had driven off The Vista's property on Monday, Kate was too upset and shaken to confront Ralph with what she had discovered. However, she could not bring herself to share the bed with him and slept on the sofa, claiming stomach problems and needing to use the restroom often during the night.

By Wednesday, a confrontation could no longer be avoided and it took place in Ralph's study.

When her husband wanted to know what exactly was wrong with her, Kate pointed to his computer monitor and exploded, "You are a sick bastard!"

"So you know - - - what exactly do you know?" Ralph stuttered.

"I know enough!"

"I can explain."

"There is nothing to explain. I saw the horrible scene on that video. Stupid me, all the time when you vanished to your precious study, I assumed you were playing computer games. Oh boy, was I ever wrong!"

"I happened upon the site by accident one day and, before I knew what was happening, I was hooked."

Kate's rage was even stronger as she stated, "There is no excuse for it. You are a disgusting bastard! Pornography in itself is bad enough, but when it involves children, it's not only revolting but also a crime."

"I'm going to stop, I swear. I'll even go for counseling if I have to," he pleaded.

Trembling, Kate cried out, "You are making me truly sick to my stomach!"

That said, she walked out of the study and slammed the door shut behind her.

CHAPTER 50

Tim's parents took their son's ashes with them to Florida, but before they left, they attended a memorial tribute for him, arranged by Amanda and held on Saturday, July 26. All the other people in attendance were friends of Tim and Amanda, for the most part UCLA students or recent graduates. It was held at an outdoor food court on campus, and even one of Tim's former professors was present.

It was a sad gathering indeed. On an easel stood an enlarged picture of Tim, enjoying his favorite activity, riding a bicycle. An array of flowers and other mementos placed around it by his friends served as a tribute. Some of the young people shared a few anecdotes they had experienced with Tim, but most mourned him quietly.

Sheriff Shaft happened upon the scene by pure chance and looked on from afar. After the event was over, he watched as Amanda said good-bye to Tim's folks and offered flowers to the mourners to take away.

She was about to put the place back in order when the sheriff stepped forward, saying, "Let me help you."

"Oh, Sheriff Shaft! What are you doing here?"

"I'm doing a little college touring with our oldest son. He's a high school senior and has been accepted by a few universities but has a hard time making up his mind about which one to commit to. He's checking out the library, the gym, and the pool on this campus right now."

They folded up the easel together and gathered everything else Amanda had brought along, plus things other people had left. They stashed the items away in her four large tote bags and carried all to her Toyota, which was parked in the nearest lot.

She said, "Thanks so much. I would have had to make two trips without your help."

The sheriff dismissed it with a casual wave of his hand. Then he said, "When I called you the other day with the news of Enzo Castelli's arrest, I was in a hurry and didn't go into details. The only things I informed you of was that he was your boyfriend's murderer, that he also turned out to be the Southland Torcher, and that we found the murder weapon. If you have time, I'll fill you in now."

She beamed and stated, "I'll make time!"

"Let's go back to the food court, where my son will meet me in about an hour."

CHAPTER 51

Amanda and the sheriff had the outdoor food court practically to themselves on a late Saturday afternoon.

Settled on a couple of chairs, facing one another, Amanda said, "You told me that Enzo's DNA matched the DNA found on the trekking poles he had used and that traces of Tim's blood were on one of the poles. But how did you arrive at suspecting him of the crime to begin with?"

"That was a long process, and not too complicated, once I started looking in the right direction," he replied.

"Here goes: I knew all along that I had missed an important fact but couldn't recall what it was. Last Sunday, during a beach outing with my wife, a chance remark she made finally got me on the right track. She said that she'd eat 'half a sandwich.' At the time I answered her with a corny remark. The half sandwich thing re-entered my brain a day or so later, when I remembered Enzo saying in his interview that he initially only ate part of his lunch and saved the rest for later. During his questioning I thought he was just being thorough, but on that later day, after it came to mind again, I made it my business to go over the notes you had taken once more and concentrated on Enzo's statements.

"He had actually mentioned the lunch thing again later in his testimony, saying that he skipped his plan to eat the rest of his sandwich when he saw a helicopter approaching. Why bring up an unimportant thing about where and when he ate his lunch, I asked myself. Must have felt important to him, I deduced. And then I remembered what a friend of mine, who is an arson investigator, once told me. He had stated that an addicted arsonist will get his kicks by watching his handiwork and celebrate after setting the fire.

"What if Enzo was the Southland Torcher and had planned to eat the rest of his lunch to celebrate and watch the blaze, but didn't get around to it because he was discovered by Tim in the act of setting it?"

"Wow! You figured all that from a two-part lunch," Amanda remarked.

"I know it wasn't much, but it got me scrutinizing the rest of his statement. And there I found the huge blunder he made and the thing that had been nagging at me subconsciously all along. He claimed to have been studying caterpillars on the sagebrush bushes during the crucial time."

The sheriff held his pointer finger up in the air for emphasis and continued, "You and I both know where those bushes are located. They are close by the trail leading up the little hill where Tim was riding his bicycle."

"Oh!" Amanda cried out, "He didn't say that he saw Tim riding up."

"Exactly! And he should have seen him from the spot where he claimed to have been. But let's say that he was too busy studying the critters and didn't look up from his task."

"In that case he would have at least seen Tim coming back down," she said. "Or did he make the whole thing about his caterpillar hobby up?"

"No. The study of caterpillars turning into butterflies is his hobby, that's a fact. But he was not seen by anyone else hanging out at those sagebrush bushes. Remember Mai Bong's testimony? She saw Tim riding up that hill after she had turned her car around at the dead end. When I asked her if she saw anyone else, she answered in the negative. But Enzo supposedly was looking at caterpillars on the sagebrush bushes. One of the two was lying, and I felt sure it was not Mai. There could only be one reason why Enzo lied about spending time inspecting those bushes. He had in fact hiked up that hill and was setting the fire on the other side."

The sheriff continued, "He made additional blunders. Telling me about packing a magnifier should have given him away, but like everyone else, I associated it with his hobby."

"I don't get it. What about the magnifier?"

"He started the fires with it."

"I don't understand."

"Done expertly, a fire can be started by aligning a magnifier with the sun. That explains why Enzo was not caught until now. There had been no evidence to be found by the arson investigators."

The sheriff went on, "He thought he was smart by telling me that he used trekking poles on his hike, just in case someone else would mention the fact. As it turned out, I may have never stumbled upon the murder weapon if he hadn't mentioned them."

Amenda asked, "How was it done? I mean, how did Tim end up in the lake?"

"I was getting to that. We actually have a written confession."

"So he is sorry for what he did and confessed?"

"Maybe, but most likely to get a lesser sentence. With all the DNA evidence, he knows that a conviction is evident."

Amanda fought back tears welling up and commented, "He must be aware of crime and punishment."

"Absolutely. As I mentioned, we have his confession in writing. After his arrest, against the advice of his attorney, he asked for pen and paper and he wrote down his sick, long story. I'm not going into details, just giving you the essence and what pertains to his crimes."

The sheriff cleared his throat and began, "Enzo started off by swearing that he planned for the Lake Castaic fire to be his last. He had conquered a gambling addiction and was going to quit and overcome his pyromania as well. He had been about to move to Texas where a new, crime-free life awaited him.

"Enzo mentioned in his confession that, way before he became an arsonist, he had heard that one could start a fire with a magnifier. He was curious and researched it. While tending to his caterpillar hobby one day, equipped with his magnifier, he tried it out, only to see if it was possible to start a fire in that fashion. To his amazement it worked, and before he could stop it, that first brush fire got out of hand. And at the same time he realized that he enjoyed watching the flames and the activity became an addiction.

"On the day of the blaze at Castaic Lake, he had briefly stopped by the sagebrush and noticed a couple of caterpillars, but his heart hadn't been in it. He wanted to take advantage of the sun around noon, so he trekked up the hill and was curious whether the terrain on the other side would be favorable for his purpose. As expected, there was plenty of dried-up brush and most importantly, the area below, where the blaze would be headed, was devoid of buildings and structures.

"Enzo started his handiwork with the magnifier, and as the blaze began to gain momentum, he was suddenly confronted by Tim, who sat on his bike at the top of the hill and wanted to know what the hell he was doing. Enzo tried to undo what he had set into motion, but it was too late and the fire had already taken over the area immediately below them. He pretended not to know how it had happened and told Tim that they needed to get away from the flames and call the authorities.

"Tim rode down the slope and Enzo ran behind him. Three fourths of the way down, Tim got his cell phone out of his backpack while Enzo caught up to him. Realizing that there was no way he could convince Tim or the authorities that he had started the blaze by accident, he needed to stop the young man at all costs. Without thinking of the consequences, he lashed out at him with one of the trekking poles, hitting him hard on the side of the head. The cell phone flew out of Tim's reach, landing in a bush nearby, while blood erupted from his wound and streamed down his face and into his eyes, blinding him.

"Enzo said that he watched in amazement, as he witnessed the young man riding down the rest of the trail, crossing the road, and heading straight into the lake. He said he watched as if in a dream, as first the bicycle and then Tim went under.

"Then Enzo wrote that he pulled himself together and was looking for Tim's phone among the bushes. He gave up the search when he heard sirens and saw a helicopter approaching, knowing that he needed to get out of the area immediately. Chances were that the phone would not be discovered any time soon anyway."

The sheriff noticed Amanda's wet eyes and stated, "That was a short version of his confession. He elaborated on many points and also confessed to setting the previous fires, but I gave you the most important details and facts. As to Tim's condition before he reached the water, the coroner let me know that your boyfriend was either semi-conscious or delirious before entering the lake."

He gave her a fatherly pat on the shoulder and said, "It might be a consolation to you that he didn't suffer."

Amanda asked, "There's going to be a trial?"

"Yes, but since he confessed, you may not need to testify."

"Oh, but I do want to testify," she said.

Sheriff Shaft looked her in the eye for a long moment and then stated, "I see. I do hope you'll get your wish."

Then he saw his son approaching and remarked, "The hour sure passed fast."

EPILOGUE

The lives of most guests who stayed at The Vista during that week in July were changed, either directly or indirectly.

Enzo Castelli spent the rest of his years behind bars, without the possibility of parole. While serving his life sentence, he tried to stay away from the other prisoners as much as possible. He had plenty of time for soul-searching and wrote a couple of non-fiction books. The first was about addiction in general, and his addictions in particular, and the second dealt with crime and punishment.

Vigo Castelli blamed himself for not having spotted his brother's predicament. He should have read the signs. Enzo had an addictive personality and had been down in the dumps more often than not, but when he'd overcome his gambling habit, Vigo thought he was, if not cured, at least on the mend. Relocating to Texas and starting afresh sounded like a great plan. Vigo had had no idea that his sibling was the Southland Torcher and, even more frightening, a killer. That fact would haunt him for the rest of his life.

Amanda Redding spent her senior college year at a university in Pisa, Italy, as planned. She enjoyed every moment of it. As a matter of fact, European life suited her. In due course, she married an Italian man and never moved back to the United States.

Jaqueline Blanchet did some major soul searching. What her friend had said while they sunbathed at the Castaic swim beach -- "Stop taking your job home with you" -- had made a major impact on her. Worrying about people in her care and their problems had kept her awake night after night for months. She was aware that it was getting worse. The time had come to change careers. Despite the tragedy experienced while staying at The Vista, Jaqueline had been impressed with the place and was drawn to a bed and breakfast endeavor. She thought about it at length. She enjoyed cooking and did not shy away from general household chores and had a hardworking person in mind whom she would hire to help with the more strenuous work. With her share of the house sale after her divorce, she was able to purchase the perfect place in Arizona, where she started her own bed and breakfast.

Clarissa Clever and Marvel Maxwell ended up dating. They alternated meeting in her town of Studio City and his of Manhattan Beach or got together somewhere in-between. Besides their strong physical attraction to one another, they truly enjoyed spending time together. Marvel admired Clarissa's sound intellect, and she appreciated his sense of humor. "He makes me laugh," she would say, if someone was curious about her male friend. As an example, Marvel called, letting her know that the malpractice lawsuit against him had ended with a hung jury and that he would be tried again. As she expressed empathy, he joked, "I'll be a whiz in the hot seat, next time around." Whether the two would end up in a permanent relationship remained to be seen.

Hien Bong gave in and saw the therapist recommended by Clarissa who, after a few sessions, made him come to terms with his problem. It turned out that his profession was not the cause of his depression but where and with whom he worked. In essence, he clashed with his boss. Hien quit his job and became an IT contractor and consultant. Ultimately, he worked for a retirement community, helping old folks manage their computers, tablets, and smartphones. Being an expert in the field, he was respected and appreciated. His depression became a thing of the past. Seeing her husband restored to his normal self made Mai happy too.

Ralph Rhymes, aka Roland Pfadfinder, retained professional help to overcome his compulsion, but as far as his wife was concerned, it was too late. She could not bring herself to look at him without disgust and filed for divorce. She basically threw him out of The Vista, and he left like a lamb.

Kate Rhymes kept the bed and breakfast going but could not do it on her own and was grateful for the help she received. The Castaic fire had been in the news for a few days and The Vista had drawn the media's attention. Rather than keeping folks away from the place, like Kate had dreaded, the opposite happened. People flocked to it and she was booked for the entire year and beyond. Human nature is a funny thing, she thought.

Martina Padilla stayed at The Vista as housekeeper. Soon after the fire and murder incident at Lake Castaic, fate was on her side. Lucky for her, but unlucky for her ex-fiancé, he was arrested for stabbing someone in a bar brawl. Not being able to come up with bail money, he was being retained. In the end, he would be tried and receive a long sentence in prison. For the first time in several months, Martina felt free as a bird and able to stay in touch with her family. Mrs. Rhymes hired her brother to take over Mr. Rhymes' duties of chauffeuring guests in the golf cart and other chores that required strength.

The Jenkins were the least affected by what had happened while they enjoyed their honeymoon. Asher worked long hours in the hope of eventually taking the senior dentist's practice over, while Norice continued working as a court reporter. She had changed from working in courts to taking depositions, which proved to be less stressful. They were a happy couple, looking forward to starting a family someday in the future.

One day in March, a year after the tragic events, they were on their way to North Shore Lake Tahoe for a well-earned ski trip. Driving north on Interstate 5 and passing Castaic Lake, Norice said to Asher, "Remember what my friend Jill, who recommended The Vista to us, said?"

"I have no idea. Refresh my memory."

"She said that the place was *a killer bed and breakfast.*"

"Jill was correct," said Asher.

Stand-Alone Mysteries by Alice Zogg

A Killer Bed & Breakfast
A Doomed Reunion
A Lethal Joke
A Dark Book Club
A Bad Apple
Exposing the Past
No Curtain Call
The Ill-Fated Scientist
Accidental Eyewitness
A Bet Turned Deadly

R. A. Huber Mysteries by Alice Zogg

Evil at Shore Haven
Guilty or Not
Murder at the Cubbyhole
Revamp Camp
Final Stop Albuquerque
The Fall of Optimum House
The Lonesome Autocrat
Tracking Backward
Turn the Joker Around
Reaching Checkmate

www.ingramcontent.com/pod-product-compliance
Lightning Source LLC
Chambersburg PA
CBHW020440180626
46812CB00003B/1323